LOLLY'S WISH

A MORGAN'S FIRE ROMANCE

M. LEE PRESCOTT

Lolly's Wish

by

M. Lee Prescott
Published by Mt. Hope Press
Copyright 2021, M. Lee Prescott
ISBN 978-1-7352948-0-3

For my family, always.

CHAPTER 1

Hands on hips, Lucy Morgan gazed at stacks of floor-to-ceiling boxes and shook her head. It was midmorning Monday, and she and her partner had been working steadily for several hours. "We really have to get a bigger office. This is getting ridiculous." She gazed over at Lolly Rogers, who had left off sorting a box of Mo Willems books and was staring into space. "What's wrong with you?"

Her friend gazed at her, a frown on her face. "I'm a hopeless case, so don't bother trying to cheer me up."

"I wasn't trying to cheer you up. I'm trying to figure out what the hell we're going to do with this mess. And you appear to be pondering the subliminal messages in the latest pigeon book," she said, referring to the character in one of the popular picture book author's series.

"Ha-ha."

"You're not a hopeless case either. Not by a long shot."

The two women owned a successful mail-order book business, Merlin's Closet, that specialized in children's books. In addition to the mail order, they ran popular book fairs in local towns and schools. Over the past two years, their business had exploded with the addition of adult mysteries to their catalogue. Their office was located on Main Street in the village of Horseshoe Crab Cove, on the second floor above Cove Toys and Games. For years, they had processed books through the office, but had recently moved overflow shipments to one of the barns at Morgan's Fire, the farm Lucy's husband, Richard, owned on the outskirts of town.

"Never mind a bigger office," Lolly said. "We need more help."

"Where would we fit another person in this rabbit warren?"

Lolly shrugged, tossing a huge ball of packing paper toward the door. "Back to my pathetic life. You have to admit, I behaved like a big girl through the wedding."

"Yes, you did. Even Richard remarked on your grace and aplomb under very trying circumstances."

The wedding in question had been at Morgan's Fire, where Lucy's stepdaughter, Pam Morgan, had married Sandy Rodriguez, Lolly's ex-husband. Lolly's had been an acrimonious divorce, with years of hurt and unresolved emotions. She'd even changed her last name from Rodriguez to Rogers, a name she'd chosen instead of keeping his name or going back to her maiden name, LaSalle.

"The mindfulness helps," Lolly said, referring to an eight-week course she'd recently completed at Cove Yoga Center. "There was so much pain, you know?"

Her friend nodded.

"I've been mostly successful in letting go."

Lucy nodded. "It's not easy."

"Wasn't Maisie the cutest flower girl?"

"The cutest. All the kids were terrific."

Lolly's eyes misted, and she set down a stack of mysteries. "That's my next hurdle."

"Oh?"

"Maisie's new mother."

"*You* are Maisie's mother, dearie. Nothing will ever change that."

"I know, but it's still hard thinking of them together. Having fun on the weekends while I sit home alone or hang out with Mother. As my dear mother loves to say, divorce is the gift that keeps on giving. Isn't that the truth?"

Lucy came to sit beside her. "I couldn't agree more. Divorce sucks, excuse my language."

Lolly put her head on her partner's shoulder. "You're one of the lucky ones. You got through it and emerged stronger and better off. Not only is Richard an amazing man, he's handsome and filthy rich."

After a painful divorce, Lucy had fallen in love with the wealthy businessman farmer and now lived at Morgan's Fire along with her two teenagers and several of her husband's adult offspring. "Yes, he's a kind, lovely man, *and* there are lots more like him out there waiting to meet *you*."

"Name one."

"Well...we might have to go a little farther afield than Horseshoe Crab Cove, but he's out there. I'm sure of it."

"Ever the optimist. At this point, I'm not even sure what I'd do with a man if I found one. I am so out of practice in the dating game. Let's get lunch and come back to this mess with renewed vigor."

"Great idea. It's such a pretty day. How about we grab sandwiches from the Café and walk down to the garden?"

Lolly hopped up, brushing cardboard bits and dust from the front of her jeans. "Sounds like a plan!"

As the friends strolled down Main Street, they were a study in contrasts. Lucy tall and slender with sky-blue eyes and shoulder-length light-brown hair and Lolly, buxom and curvaceous, with long, thick raven hair and violet eyes.

"Maybe I should cut my hair in a bob like yours. What do you think?" Lolly asked as they neared the Crab Café.

Lucy smiled. "It's your decision, but I think your hair is glorious just the way it is."

~

Jack Faulkner passed the "Welcome to Horseshoe Crab Cove" sign and wondered if he'd made a mistake. Tired of the city, he'd volunteered to spend a few weeks, maybe longer, in the village. His job

—to assess the development potential of a property in a prime location at the village's southwest corner. *Am I insane?* he mused, thinking about all the work he'd left behind. *I'll go crazy trying to catch up. Is a few weeks in the country, even beautiful country like this, worth the aggravation?*

He drove along Main Street, eyes scanning the street for the Crab Café, where he was to meet Lindsay Barnes, the Realtor handling the Barnum property. Just as he spotted the café's sign, he also spied two beautiful women heading into the restaurant, one slender, her companion full-figured. A heavy-set guy, Jack preferred a woman with curves, and this one was something! *Maybe this won't be so bad after all,* he thought, parking in a lot at the end of the street.

As he entered the café, he spied the two women waiting to order. Since no one had rushed up to greet him, he decided to make some new friends. "Hi, ladies," he said, elbow resting on the counter as he leaned forward to address them both.

They turned as one. The slender one smiled, her blue eyes warm. "Hello." Her raven-haired companion just stared at him with the most beautiful violet eyes he'd ever seen.

"I don't suppose either of you know Lindsay Barnes? I'm supposed to meet her here."

The slender woman cocked her head. "End of the counter, chatting with the waitress. You must be new in town. I'm Lucy Morgan, and this is my friend Lolly Rogers."

He grinned, extending his hand. "Jack Faulkner." They both shook his hand, but the electricity switched on when he and Ms. Rogers touched. *Hmm...*

At that moment, a petite blonde in a red business suit, crisp white blouse, and five-inch heels stepped between Jack and the two women. "Mr. Faulkner?"

He nodded.

"Lindsay Barnes. Welcome to Horseshoe Crab Cove."

"Hello. Thanks for meeting me, Ms. Barnes," he said, extending his hand. Even with her heels, he towered over her. Early forties, he guessed. Her pixie haircut suited her, the gobs of makeup not so much. "These kind ladies had just pointed you out."

"Hey, gals," she said, giving Lucy and Lolly a quick glance before returning her green eyes to the handsome newcomer. "I see you've met our booksellers, two of the town's most successful businesswomen."

Lolly guffawed. "Hardly."

Jack turned to her. "Oh? Where's your bookshop? I'd like to stop in and grab some reading material for my visit." *This woman has the most amazing eyes. Liz Taylor had nothing on Lolly Rogers.*

"No shop. We're strictly mail order. Sorry." *You don't know how sorry I am!* she thought, weak-kneed as she smiled at the handsome stranger with his broad shoulders, stocky build and sandy hair. Wire-rimmed glasses accentuated his warm blue eyes.

Lucy smiled as she watched the interplay between her friend and Jack Faulkner. "We sell children's books and a small catalog of mysteries, but Village Books is right down the street, and they have a great selection of all genres."

"Jack, why don't I find us a table?" Lindsay asked, grasping his arm.

Ignoring the Realtor, he turned to Lolly. "Adult mysteries?"

She nodded. "We pride ourselves on finding great regional mystery writers. Strong sense of place along with wonderful, intricate plotting."

He smiled, gaze lingering on her beautiful eyes. "My favorite kind. Might I get a catalog somewhere?"

Lolly blushed. "Well, we... I mean we don't... There's our website and a few upcoming bookfairs."

"I tell you what," Lucy said, reaching into her purse. "Here's our card. We're right up the street, second floor above Cove Toys and Games. We're usually in between ten and four, but I'd call ahead. We'd be happy to recommend a good mystery or two. If it's in stock, it's yours as a welcome-to-town gift. If you'll be in town awhile, we've just had two cancellations for our upcoming Mystery Weekend, in case you'd be interested in that?"

"Oh?" he said, grinning as he gazed between the two friends.

"Weekend after next," Lucy said. "We'd love to have you. Stop by the office, and we'll give you a flyer, or you can sign up on the website."

"Oh look, Jack!" Lindsay said, pulling him away. "A table has opened by the window. Shall we?"

Jack grinned holding up the card as he allowed himself to be dragged off. "Thanks. I'll be in touch!"

Their sandwiches ready, the partners took their bags and headed for the door, gazing in the direction of their recent companions. Lindsay had positioned herself so that Jack's back was to the door.

"Well, well, well," Lucy said as they stepped out. "That was interesting."

Lolly shrugged. "What are you talking about?"

Lucy paused on the sidewalk, laughing. "You know darn well what I'm talking about. Mr. Tall, Dark, and Handsome?"

Lolly smiled. "Not too tall, light hair, but you're right...*very* handsome. Men like that are attracted to women like you and Lindsay Barnes, not dumpy old me."

"Don't be ridiculous. Jack Faulkner couldn't be less interested in Lindsay or me. He only had eyes for you, my dear. Gorgeous blue eyes, I might add."

"He was just being polite. Now let's go. I'm starving."

"If that was polite, I can't wait to see when your Mr. Faulkner really turns on the charm."

"Ha-ha. He is not *my* Mr. Faulkner, and I doubt we'll ever see him again. I wonder why he's here anyway. What would he want with Lindsay? Why didn't we think to ask?"

"Hmm... If you're interested, I can tap into the village grapevine. I'm sure there'll be chatter by tonight."

"Very funny," Lolly said, smiling as she led the way into Laura's Community Garden. "There's a bench in the shade. Come on."

CHAPTER 2

Jack whistled as he and Lindsay stood on the porch of Barnum's Ledge, the three-story inn at the southwest corner of Horseshoe Crab Cove.

"Some view, isn't it?" she asked. In front of them, Mount Hope Bay sparkled. As far as the eye could see, blue waves crested as the wind picked up.

"View's terrific. Building will have to be gutted, cottages too."

They'd spent the last hour touring the property, which consisted of the huge Victorian main building, six guest cottages, two barns, and several smaller outbuildings. The Barnum family had moved away a decade earlier, leaving a caretaker tasked to maintain the place. He'd basically done nothing. When the disrepair came to the attention of the town manager, he contacted the Barnum family, who were now spread all over the country.

Finger to her lips, Lindsay assumed a pensive look. "Oh, I don't know. Surely some of the cottages can be refurbished with a good contractor, maybe the inn too? I know a few excellent contractors."

Jack smiled. "We'd bring our people in for this."

"Oh, well...of course," she said, not quite successful in keeping the pique from her voice. "So what's our next step?"

"I'll bring a team down to go over everything. Should be able to get my people here tomorrow morning. Would you have free time?"

She smiled, leaning into him. "For you, anytime." Lindsay had been flirting since they met in the Café, but Jack was definitely not interested. Still it didn't hurt to play along if it meant a better sale price.

"Basically, we'd be buying the land," he said. "I hope the owners know that."

"None of them have been back in years. They remember its heyday. Until your company contacted me, they hadn't even entertained selling. They may be very attached and not ready to just let it go."

"Uh-huh," Jack said drily, as he pointed to the rotting porch floor. "Well, if they haven't seen any recent photos, I'd suggest you take some or I can have my crew take some. If we decide to make an offer, we *all* want to be realistic."

"Of course," she said. "Not sure what your plans are, but I have a client meeting in half an hour. I could call the office and ask one of my associates to take that meeting, if you'd like to grab a drink or dinner?"

"Thanks, but I'd like to get settled in." At her suggestion, he'd contacted Mavis LaSalle, who owned a large property east of town that included a spa and event venue. One of Mavis's three cottages had been available.

"Oh, that's right, you're out at Mavis's, aren't you?" Lindsay neglected to mention that one of the women he'd been so interested in at the Café earlier lived on the estate, Lolly Rogers, Mavis's eldest daughter.

"Yup. Looking forward to using the gym and spa."

"Hmm, I wonder if you might be more comfortable in town? I don't know why I didn't suggest the Blueberry B and B. It's charming and right up Beach Road from here. You could stroll down and poke around anytime."

"Thanks, but I'll be fine. I'm not much of a B and B man. Besides, my assistant called ahead and had them stock the cottage with food and drink. I'll be all set."

"Well... If you're sure?"

"Absolutely. Shall we?" He gestured toward the driveway. "Don't want you to be late to your meeting."

As Jack turned onto Main Street, he saw the sign for Village Toys and Games, then checked his watch. Three fifteen. On impulse, he pulled into a space on the street and hopped out. *I feel like a good regional mystery. Let's see if those intriguing ladies are in.*

When he reached the second-floor hall, he faced a wall of doors, none marked until he reached the far end. A small sign reading "Merlin's Closet" was on the wall to the left of the door. He knocked and heard a voice call, "Come in!"

A wall of boxes greeted him, with no one in sight. He called, "Hello?"

She poked her head around the box wall. "Oh!" Then disappeared. "Hold on a sec."

Lolly hopped up, vainly endeavoring to smooth her hair. When she emerged, wiping dirty hands on her jeans, she still had smudges of dust on her nose and cheeks. "We're not... I mean we don't... Lucy's gone home. It's just me here." *Why am I suddenly speaking like a blithering idiot?*

Jack smiled, stepping around stacks of books as he came closer. She looked adorable covered in dust. "I thought I'd stop in and see if you had a book to recommend?"

"Well... It might be tricky. We've been unpacking all day." Lolly felt faint and tongue-tied. *What is it about this stranger?*

"I'm not picky," he said, pulling a handkerchief out of his pocket and leaning forward to touch her nose and cheeks.

Must be the last man on earth to carry a cloth handkerchief, she thought, grabbing it and furiously wiping her face. "Oh, gee, thanks. I'm sure I look like a fright, covered in dirt."

Like a deer in the headlights. "I think you got it all. And you look just fine from where I'm standing."

"Thank you," she said, handing him the dirty handkerchief. "So what kinds of mysteries do you like?"

"Not too fond of cozies. Anything else is fine."

"Hmm... Most of the regionals tend toward the cozy," she said, attempting to keep her voice light and breezy. "Do you know Sally Gunning's work? Her 'water mysteries' are set in a Cape Cod-like area."

"Don't know her, but I'll take one or two. Do you have the first couple in the series?"

"That might take me a few minutes. Feel free to sit, if you can find a place."

Jack leaned against a desk covered with papers and books. *What a perfect round ass*, he thought, watching her move boxes aside, then stoop to search the bottom shelf of a long bookcase.

When she stood up and turned, two paperbacks in hand, Lolly knew very well what he'd been doing. Brushing hair from her face, she stepped over some book piles, then handed him the novels. "Here you go. These should get you started. If you don't like the first, you can always return the second."

"How much do I owe you?"

"Well... I... We don't usually, actually ever, sell out of the office. I could... Oh, what the heck. Take 'em."

"I couldn't."

"You could. As Lucy said, you can consider them a welcome-to-town gift." Feeling wobbly and strangely overheated, Lolly leaned on a stack of boxes. Before she knew it, the stack tilted, taking her with it.

Jack grabbed her arm with one hand, the other reaching around to catch the topmost box before the pile toppled. "Whoa, Nellybelle."

Before she knew it, they were pressed against each other, Jack fighting to keep them upright. He smelled of spices and the sea, his strong chest crushing her breasts. Breathless, Lolly wondered if she might faint or swoon. Inwardly shaking herself, she thought, *Get a grip, girl! If this is what a man does to you, you've got to get out there and start dating again.*

Suddenly, she laughed. "Nellybelle?"

He grinned. "You're probably too young to remember Roy Rogers. Before my time too. Just slipped out in the heat of the moment."

Heat. You've got that right, she thought. "My Dad was obsessed with that old show. Had us watching it with him all the time growing up."

Gently, he let her go. "Hey how 'bout I buy you a drink to pay for the books? Is there a place nearby?"

"Thanks, ordinarily I'd love to, but I've got to pick up my daughter. Oh gee, look at the time. Gotta get moving."

"Another time, then?"

Too tongue-tied to speak, she nodded, grabbing her bag.

They walked out together. "Can I walk you to your car?" he asked.

"Where are you parked?"

He pointed to his SUV. "Just there."

"Well, you go on. I'm up the street. See ya!"

Lolly turned and jogged up the street to the lot alongside Averill's Store. *What is the matter with you?* she thought. *You didn't ask where he's staying, what he's doing here or how long he'll be around! Stupid, stupid, stupid!*

Jack watched her go, realizing he hadn't asked where she lived, how old her daughter was, her phone number? Nothing. *You're losing your touch, buddy.*

HE DROVE OUT OF TOWN AND TURNED IN AT THE SIGN THAT READ COVE Inn and Spa, passing by the main house, Netherfield Manor, and two other tree-lined lanes on his way through the property until he reached a dirt road with a small sign announcing Osprey Cottage on the fence rail.

Mavis LaSalle had left the cottage open, keys on the kitchen counter. *Perfect,* he thought, gazing around the two-bedroom house, which was nestled in the trees at the end of the long narrow lane. It was exquisitely furnished in muted colors, with comfortable upholstered chairs and sofas, tasteful artwork on the walls, wrought iron lamps, and antique dining table and chairs.

After setting his suitcases down in the larger bedroom, he decided to explore the grounds before unpacking. There were several paths around the cottage, and he decided to take the east one, hoping to catch a glimpse of the shore and river. As he set off across the lawn, he heard voices and laughter behind him. He turned to spy a pretty dark-haired child emerging from the woods and chattering to someone behind her. As Jack paused, the girl, who appeared to be about six or seven, squinted and adjusted her glasses, her chocolate-brown eyes wide. "Mommy, there's a man in the field."

Her companion came into view. "What'd you say, baby?"

Lolly Rogers ruffled her daughter's curls, then looked up. "Oh, it's you!"

CHAPTER 3

Jack grinned as he approached mother and child. "What a nice surprise. Do you live nearby?"

Lolly met his deep-blue eyes. "You could say that. What are you doing here?" Flustered and blushing, she wasn't entirely successful in keeping the edge out of her voice.

He waved an arm behind him. "I've rented this amazing cottage for a few weeks, maybe longer. And who is this beautiful young lady?"

"Maisie, this is Mr. Faulkner."

Her daughter stared up at him, smiling. "Hi."

"Hi yourself," he said, extending his hand, which she took, giving him a firm handshake. He wasn't exaggerating. She was one of the prettiest children he'd ever seen, with her sparkling chocolate-brown eyes. He wondered about her father. "I was just going out for a walk. Don't suppose you ladies would like to show me around? I was hoping to find the river. Will that path take me there?"

"Sure will," Maisie said, jumping up and down. "Can we show him, Mommy? Can we?"

"Okay, precious, but not too far. We promised Grandma we'd be there soon."

Jack bowed and gestured toward the east path. "Lead on, ladies."

Maisie skipped on ahead, and he followed her mother, marveling at her round, perfect ass in those tight, sexy jeans. She'd changed from their earlier encounter and now wore a tan canvas jacket and sneakers, her long hair in a ponytail that swished as she walked.

As they reached a wider point in the path, he came alongside her, Maisie out of view around the next bend. "So did I interrupt an 'over the river and through the woods, to Grandmother's house we go' moment?"

"Sort of, but we were planning to take a beach walk first. Mavis is my mother. We live in one of the other cottages, just through the woods."

Jack grinned, shaking his head. "Funny that Lindsay didn't mention the connection when we met today. She's the one who booked me in here."

Lolly smiled. "Sounds like she may have a crush on you."

"She's got a crush on anyone who she thinks will make her money."

"Is that why you're here? To buy property?"

"Maybe. The old Barnum place. Do you know it?"

"I love that place. When we...I first moved back to town, my ex-husband and I considered buying and restoring it."

As they walked, they brushed against each other, a sensation he found more than a little arousing. *Down, boy!* "Oh? What stopped you?"

"He was more interested in starting a music venue than us being innkeepers."

"A music venue around here?"

"Go figure. It's one of the most successful of its type on the East Coast. Can you see Maisie? I better check," she said, breaking into a jog.

Jack followed, appreciating his companion's athletic prowess as he struggled to keep pace. They spied her around the next turn. Just ahead, she was scrambling up a large boulder, the shoreline in front of her.

"Maisie, be careful!" her mother cried. The warning was largely unnecessary as her daughter appeared surefooted and steady.

"You remind me of a mountain goat!" he said, watching as her mother joined her on the top of the rock. His six-hundred-dollar shoes, Churches, were not exactly suited for climbing. *Why didn't I change into sneakers for a beach walk? What the hell. Let's hope I don't kill myself.* He slowly edged his way up to the top, finally flopping down beside them.

"What a view," he said, gazing downward. The craggy embankment plunged to a narrow stretch of beach below. "You and the mountain goat aren't considering climbing down this way, are you?"

Lolly chuckled. "Not unless we're crazy, which we aren't. Are we, Maise?"

Her daughter threw her head back, laughing, "Silly. Come on, the path's this way." She scooted down the boulder on her bottom and leapt off to a dirt path running north through the thicket.

Lolly followed, then turned back, reaching toward him. "Need a hand?"

Jack started to protest , then grinned. "What the heck. Not often I get rescued by a beautiful woman." Even though he could have managed easily, he grasped her hand, edging down to stand beside her, their bodies inches apart. "Thanks," he said, still holding her hand.

Paralyzed, Lolly turned crimson. Finally, she shook herself, withdrawing her hand. "Didn't want you to ruin those fancy shoes." As she turned and hurried after Maisie, her whole body tingled from head to toe.

Jack stood for a few seconds, stunned at his own body's reaction to a woman he'd met only a few hours earlier. *This wasn't in the plan for the next few weeks, especially on the heels of Marsha. This trip is supposed to be a getaway, a chance to uncomplicate my life, get immersed in a new project. Slow down, buddy!*

"Come on, Jack," a tiny voice called, and he hurried along the well-worn path to the beach below.

~

"THIS IS INCREDIBLE," HE SAID AS HE KICKED OFF HIS SHOES AND SOCKS and waded into the water alongside them. "Reminds me of the Maine shoreline."

"You're from Maine?"

"Summered there for a time."

"Whereabouts?"

"Small island off Boothbay Harbor. My wife's family owned several houses there."

"Oh... You're married. Of course you are."

He grinned, pleased at her reaction. *She's interested in you, buddy. You haven't lost your touch.* "Ex-wife."

Maisie squealed, splashing beside her. "Horseshoe crabs! Look, Mommy, look, Jack!"

They gazed down to spy two crabs, a smaller one attached to a larger one as they swam along the sandy bottom.

Maisie pointed. "That's the daddy in the back."

"The little one?" he said.

The child nodded. "Yup."

"It's mating season," Lolly said.

"They're sure weird-looking creatures, aren't they?"

"They've been around since the dinosaurs," Maisie said. "They're the coolest animals in the world."

"Wow, I didn't know that."

"My Uncle Tim rescues them."

Lolly opened her mouth to correct her, then realized that Tim Miller, now married to Gail Morgan, sister to her ex-husband's new wife, Pam, was indeed her uncle. A wave of sadness washed over her thinking about the huge new family of which her sweet baby was now a part. *A family that doesn't include me.*

Jack glimpsed the sadness in her lovely eyes. "You okay?"

Lolly shook herself. "Fine. She's talking about her dad's brother-in-law, Tim. He's a part-time lobsterman who also patrols the coastline and reports crab poachers. They've decimated the horseshoe crab population over the years. They catch them for bait. There's a moratorium on them now, but the poachers persist. It's easy money, if they can get away with it."

"They're bad people," the child said.

Jack frowned. "Sure are. Lucky thing these guys are free and having a good ole time."

"Oh, gee, look at the time!" Lolly said, gazing at her watch. "Come on, Maise, we've gotta head up to Grandma's."

"Can I walk with you?" he said.

Caught off guard by the question, she turned to him. "Sure... Okay... Actually, it's the most direct route back to where you're staying."

"Come on, Jack!" Maisie called, already running along the beach toward another path that led up the cliffs.

A short walk brought them to the back lawn of Netherfield Manor, Mavis LaSalle's massive home and inn. The mansion and grounds reminded Jack of Newport's Cliff Walk and the huge "cottages" that lined the historic path. He whistled. "Pretty impressive."

"Welcome to Netherfield, Mother's masterpiece. It wasn't always so grand. In fact, it wasn't unlike the current state of Barnum's Ledge when she bought it. She's a Jane Austen fanatic, hence the name."

As they neared the home, a slender dark-haired sixty-something woman waved, rising from her seat on the terrace and coming down to greet them. "Hi, precious!" she called as Maisie ran to hug her. "Snacks and lemonade on the terrace."

When she straightened up, gazing at her daughter and her companion, Jack saw where Lolly had gotten her remarkable eyes.

"Who have you brought to dinner, my dear?"

"Mother, this is your tenant, Jack Faulkner. I take it you two haven't met?"

"No, but what a lovely surprise," she said, coming forward to shake his hand. "Have you just arrived, then?"

He nodded. "'Bout an hour ago. Very nice to meet you, Ms. LaSalle."

"Mavis, dear. Is the cottage okay?"

"Perfect. What a property this is."

"We like it, don't we, honey?" she asked, gazing over at her daughter.

Lolly nodded.

"Well," Jack said, "I'd better get going. Don't want to disturb your dinner. I think I can find my way back from here."

"Nonsense!" his host said, waving her hand. "You will join us for dinner unless you have other plans? My chef always makes enough to feed an army."

Jack glanced over at Lolly, who shrugged. "Your choice. Kendall's cooking is to die for."

He grinned. "In that case, I would be honored. Thank you."

Mavis took his arm. "No, thank you, dear Jack. It's not often that we have such a handsome man to grace our table."

Here we go, Lolly thought, following the pair onto the terrace.

CHAPTER 4

Mavis's chef, Kendall Reese, had prepared skewers of swordfish and vegetables served over a saffron rice, asparagus, and beautiful summer salads of field greens, luscious tomatoes, and nasturtium flowers. To Jack's surprise, Maisie happily devoured her meal, chattering away the entire time. "Your daughter has a sophisticated palate," Jack said as Maisie told her grandmother about the horseshoe crab sighting.

"Always has. She never tasted baby food. We just mushed up what we were having, and she ate it."

As Maisie finished her story, Mavis gazed at her companions. "So, Jack, what brings you to our quaint little village? The agent who booked the cottage didn't say."

"I'm looking at property for my company. The old Barnum place."

"How exciting. I've always had my eye on that. Even Lolly thought about it once upon a time. Did she tell you?"

He watched Lolly's face cloud over. "She did. This is an incredible meal."

Mavis waved her hand toward the kitchen. "Our Kendall is the best chef in New England, maybe the country."

"Aren't you fortunate," he said, as Lolly rolled her eyes.

"Grandma, can I go help Kendi?" Maisie said

"Of course precious. So...tell us about yourself, Jack dear. Are you married? Children? Where do you live?"

"Divorced, two kids, but at twenty and eighteen, not kids anymore. They're both in college. I live in Boston. They alternate their time at home between my place and their mother's. They prefer her family's house in Maine in the summer over condo living, I'm afraid."

"Divorce can be so heart-wrenching, can it not? We three should know." Mavis gestured around the table before taking a sip of the excellent chardonnay Kendall had served with the fish.

He nodded, aware that Lolly hadn't uttered a word. "You make it work for the kids."

"Of course you do. I know I tried with my four."

"Big family," he said.

"There are a lot of those in Horseshoe Crab Cove," Lolly said, gazing at her mother. "In fact, ours would be considered on the skimpy side with only four."

"Does all your family live around here?" he asked.

"Heavens, no. My oldest, Duncan, is in California, and Dara, my second child, lives in Paris. Lolly's younger sister, Marla, is in a musical group. They're based here, but they're frequently on tour somewhere, aren't they, sweetie?"

Lolly smiled, directing her reply to him. "Mostly local touring. She lives in Bayport, about twenty minutes from here."

"What kind of music?"

Lolly folded her napkin by her side, aware of her mother's eagle eyes trained on her. "Bluegrass, folk."

"Love bluegrass. Are they any good?"

Lolly nodded. "They're pretty popular."

"Not my kind of music," her mother said, "but we have booked them for weddings when the couple wants that kind of music."

"Love to hear them while I'm in town. Do you know if they have any gigs the next few weeks?"

Mavis stood. "As a matter of fact, Marla just dropped off her latest tour schedule. I believe they're playing at Sandy's sometime soon. Let me get the brochure."

As Mavis disappeared, he said, "I think I passed that place, Sandy's? Is it on the coast road?"

"Can't miss it."

"You okay?" She didn't look okay. In fact she looked as if she were preparing for dental surgery.

Before Lolly could answer, her mother reappeared, waving a flyer. "I was right. They'll be at Sandy's this Friday night. You take this, dear. Maybe Lolly will take you? She doesn't often frequent the place except when our Marla is playing."

Before he could ask why not, Maisie opened the kitchen door. "Ta-dah! We're having floating island, my favorite!"

As the trio said their goodbyes and strolled down the manor drive, fingers of orange and pink covered the western sky. "Look at that sunset," he said. "Don't see that in the city."

"It's pretty much like that every night, but this is an extra cool one, I admit."

Jack pointed to Maisie as she skipped in front of them, trying to catch fireflies. "Not to mention those. Lightning bugs?"

Lolly smiled. "Or fireflies. An author I love describes them as the stars coming down from the sky."

"Lovely." *As are you.* "So what do you say? Are you up for accompanying me to your sister's gig?"

"Usually a group of us go, my partner Lucy, her husband, whoever we can corral."

There was a stiffness to her voice, a reserve that hadn't been there earlier. "Sounds fun."

She shrugged. "I go to support my sister."

"Must be tough."

"Excuse me?"

"That place? Sandy's? It's your ex-husband's business. Isn't it?"

"Was. He sold it earlier this year for a ridiculous amount of money."

"But they kept the name?"

"Wouldn't be Sandy's without it. Now can we change the subject, please?"

"Only if you agree to have dinner with me tomorrow night."

"Didn't we just make a date for Friday?"

He grinned, gazing over at her. "Date? I like the sound of that."

Glad of the growing darkness to hide her red cheeks, Lolly waved her hand, accidently brushing against his arm, and electricity coursed through her. "You know what I mean."

"Sure do." His grin widened. "Dinner? Tomorrow? You name the time and place."

"I don't know... It is Maisie's night with her dad, but—"

"Come on. It's just dinner, not a marriage proposal. I don't know anyone in town. You can give me the lowdown while we eat."

"I guess it'd be okay, but let me confirm with my ex and let you know, okay?"

"Great. I'll plan on picking you up at seven, but here's my card with my cell number if anything changes. If you lose it, Lindsay has it too."

Lolly took the business card, pausing. "This is you." They stood at the top of the drive leading to his cottage.

"Wouldn't be very gallant if I didn't walk you home."

"Our driveway's right up there, and my mother gave Maisie a flashlight. Besides, our road is much shorter. We'd walk you home, but I don't like to tromp through the woods path after dark with Maisie."

"Critters?"

"Coyotes. Maisie, hold up! Come say good night to Jack!" she called.

Her daughter waved, already fifty yards ahead. "Bye, Jack!"

"Night," he called, waving. "Come visit anytime!"

"Don't encourage her."

"It's fine, really. I love kids."

Lolly found his nearness alternatively comforting and terrifying. *What in the world is happening here?* she wondered. "Well, good night."

He leaned forward and gave her a hug that lasted a bit longer than a casual friendly embrace. "Night. Thanks for tonight. Nice to be welcomed to town. Feels like I've been here for years." His soft voice caressed her neck.

Flustered, Lolly pushed back, the scent of sandalwood and spices lingering. "Great, fine, night." With that, she turned and hurried off to catch up with Maisie. *One more second and I'd have dragged him into the bushes!*

Jack watched until they disappeared in the darkness, then turned and strolled down the cottage drive, the flashlight on his smart phone lighting the way as he mused about how intoxicating her scent of honeysuckle and lemon was when he held her. *This is the last thing you need right now, buddy*, he thought, scanning the underbrush for creatures. *But how can I turn my back on the most interesting woman I've ever met?*

He breathed a sigh of relief when he spied the light in the cottage, thankful he'd thought to switch it on before his walk. As he clicked off his phone, a shadow passed by the side of the house, and Jack hurried inside.

CHAPTER 5

On the office floor, papers and books surrounding her, Lolly looked up at her friend. "I know nothing about him. He's only in town for a few weeks, then he'll be gone."

Hands on hips, Lucy gazed down at her, smiling. "It's one dinner. He's a gorgeous single guy who's magically dropped in your lap. Why not have some fun? Besides, if you hit it off, who's to say he'll disappear?"

"The last gorgeous guy who dropped in my lap broke my heart."

"Jack Faulkner is not Sandy Rodriguez. Besides, you're older and wiser. You can handle yourself."

"Says you. I haven't been with a man in so long, I don't know what I might do. What if I freak out? If Maisie hadn't been with us last night, I'd have been tempted to throw myself at him. It's unnerving."

"Sounds very promising to me!" Lucy sang, dancing around the room.

"Ha-ha, and watch out you don't trip. We've really got to find a bigger space."

"I agree. Maybe Jack could ask Lindsay if she's got any rental properties."

"Maybe *we* could ask around, thank you," Lolly said, throwing a ball of brown wrapping paper at her. "Now let's get cracking."

"Not until you call and confirm with Jack."

"We said seven tonight."

"Just make sure. Call and then it will be settled so you can stop fretting about it. I need your full attention today."

"Sandy's got Maisie now, and he was supposed to have her tonight, but something's come up and he changed days on me. I need a sitter. Is Amy available? I mean, I can ask Mother, but the less she knows about my business, the better."

"I'll call her." Lucy grabbed her cell phone and punched in her daughter's number. "Hey, sweetie, you free tonight? Lolly needs a sitter. Great... I'll tell her." Lucy gazed over at her partner. "Time?"

"Six forty-five?"

Lucy chatted for a few minutes, then rang off. "She's all set. She's at her dad's tonight, so he'll drop her at your place." Lucy's ex-husband, Rob, lived in their former home, his family home, in Somers, just a short drive from the center of Horseshoe Crab Cove. "Maybe Jack could give her a lift back?"

"That's asking a lot."

"Rob will pick her up, or her brother can. No worries. Now call him!"

Jack stood on the ledge in front of the inn, his foreman at his side. "What do you think, Pete?"

Just as Pete Santoro started to speak, Jack's phone rang, and he put up a finger. The number was unfamiliar, but he picked anyway. "Hello?"

"Hi, it's me," she said, voice tentative.

He almost said, *Who's me?* but decided to skip the wisecrack. "Morning. I was hoping to hear from you."

"Yes...well, I...I'm calling to confirm about dinner. If you're still free?"

"Absolutely."

"I was going to suggest Bluewater. It's a casual place just south of town. Great seafood."

"Sound greats. Seven still work?"

"Yes, fine."

"Perfect. I'll pick you up at seven."

As he said goodbye and clicked off, he noticed Lindsay at his side. "Hot date?" she asked.

He chuckled, gazing first at Pete, then the Realtor. "Something like that. Come on, Pete, let's see what the guys have discovered about the foundation."

One of crew, finish carpenter Ray Solomos, shook his head as he spied Jack descending the basement stairs. "It's gonna need work, boss. Sills are rotted in places, termites, water damage, you name it."

With Lindsay at his back navigating the steps in her five-inch heels, Jack didn't want to get into a serious conversation about renovation. Instead, he winked at Ray. "So you're saying tear down?"

The wiry carpenter gazed from Jack to Pete, then said, "Yeah, prob'ly."

Jack had no intention of tearing the beautiful building down, but wanted to assess the situation in private before making Compass's offer. The woodwork alone was priceless and, if restored, would make this a showplace. That was, if *his* bosses agreed.

"Okay, well, let's head into town, get your guys some lunch." He turned to Lindsay, who had finally reached them and now held fast to the stair rail to steady herself. "Thanks for your time, Lindsay. It's gonna take us a few days to get the offer ready."

Her face fell, but she straightened her shoulders and flicked a tuft of hair from her forehead. "Of course. Just to let you know, there are other interested parties."

He was pretty sure she was bluffing, but he'd already fallen in love with the property. *Or is it the village and a certain resident that I've fallen for?* Either way, he could bluff or strong arm with the best of them. "This is a problem, Linds. I can't ask my guys to spend days estimating the job only to find out the property's been sold. Doing a feasibility study takes time."

"I totally understand," she said, leaning into him. "But the Barnums are eager to move forward."

Yesterday, the Barnums hadn't even been contemplating selling, he thought, but said nothing. "After you, milady," he said, gesturing toward the stairs.

As they stood in the drive chatting, he said, "I'd like forty-eight hours exclusive." *Then all the other mythical buyers can swoop in.*

She gazed up at him. "Well...that's a bit irregular."

"Not on projects of this scale."

She took a step back, hand on hip, and smiled. "Projects can move forward without a sale."

"True, but I can offer you and the family ten grand to wait two days. After that, money's released and all your other buyers can start a bidding war. Right now, we're looking at a wreck and need time to assess feasibility."

"I'll check with my manager and the Barnums and get back to you, shall I?"

"That'd be great. Thanks, Linds."

As the Realtor drove off in her cherry red Miata, Pete whistled. "You sure fed her a load of bullshit, didn't you, boss?"

Jack chuckled. "Yeah, I did, didn't I? Let's go eat." Remembering the Crab Café crowd, Jack suggested they head to a diner on Bayport Road. That way, the crew could head home from there.

CHAPTER 6

After a long day at work, Lolly headed for her ex-husband's house on Beach Road. Sandy's truck and Audi were parked in the drive, but not his new wife's Forrester. She parked on the street and knocked at the front door. From this side, the house appeared modest, its barn-board siding bleached gray and simple. Lolly noticed planters had been added on either side of the entry, flowering shrubs in each. *The wife's idea?*

"Hey," he said, startling her as he swung open the door. With his coal-black bedroom eyes and gorgeous body, Sandy Rodriguez could always take her breath away. Today was no exception.

"She ready?" Lolly asked, stepping inside.

"Hi, Mommy!" a voice called from upstairs.

"She's getting dressed. We were in the river, swimming and crabbing. She's had a shower." He ushered her back to the kitchen and family room with its high ceilings, state-of-the-art appliances, and spectacular views of the water.

"Great, thanks. Good day?"

"The best. Sorry about tonight. I'd have loved to have her, but there's a thing out at the farm." He referred to his in-laws' home, Morgan's Fire, Richard Morgan's huge farm on the outskirts of the village.

"No prob. Amy's sitting. Maisie loves her." Lolly gazed around, noticing new feminine touches everywhere. Colorful pillows, several new chairs, artwork, and jugs of flowers on the dining room table, the marble counter, and on the sunporch's coffee table. *A woman has moved in here*, she thought, a pang of sadness washing over her. While Sandy had moved to this house after their divorce, its stark modern look was familiar. Now it was this, a warmer home, a home filled with love. *Something else I'll have to adjust to.*

"Can I get you something to drink? Pam's just run out to the store. She'll be back soon."

"No, thanks, we've got to scoot. Maisie!" she called over her shoulder. "Hurry up, sweetie!"

As she and Maisie drove up Beach Road, they passed Pam Morgan Rodriguez's gray Subaru. "There's Pammy!" Maisie cried from the back seat, and they both waved.

At least she didn't say Mommy, Lolly thought, turning the corner onto Main Street. *Divorce. It sure is the gift that keeps on giving.*

LOLLY DRESSED CAREFULLY, CHOOSING CLOTHES THAT FLATTERED HER curvaceous figure. The soft fuchsia top, sleeveless with a vee neck draped perfectly over her full breasts, then flowed loose at her hips. Black capris and strappy sandals completed her outfit and she wore artisan jewelry of colorful beads—earrings and a necklace. Her dark hair fell in waves over her shoulders, and she applied a hint of makeup to accentuate her eyes and lips. As she twirled in front of the mirror, satisfied with her appearance, she spied Rob Brennan's car pulling into the drive. As she watched, Amy hopped out and waved, then Lucy's ex drove off. He and Lolly were not the best of friends.

"You look cool, Lolly," Amy said as she came down stairs. Maisie was curled up in the den, watching a show.

"Thanks. How are you doing, Amy?"

"Pretty well. Trying to cram in summer before I head west again." This was the second year Amy had traveled to Morgan's Run to live and work on her uncle's ranch. She was a counselor at Emma's Dream, the camp started by Ben and Maggie Morgan for handicapped children.

"Oh, that's right. When do you go?"

"Two weeks. My best friend Celia's coming this year."

"How fun is that? Where do you stay?"

"That's the coolest part. We stay with the kids, in the bunkhouses, when camp's in session, but in between when we have a weekend break, they're letting us use one of the ranch cabins."

"That'll be fun."

Amy nodded. "Can't wait," she said, gazing toward the front of the house. "I think your date just drove in."

"Friend," Lolly said. "He's just a friend."

Amy grinned. "That's what Mom said." She headed for the den to say hello to Maisie.

"Dinner's on the counter. Pizza. There's a salad in the fridge." Lolly flew in and kissed Maisie on the head. "Be good for Amy!" She was at the door as Jack reached it. "All set," she said, pushing the screen door open. His look told her she'd chosen her clothes well.

"You look lovely," he said, blue eyes taking in every inch of her.

Lolly smiled. "Thanks." *You look pretty hunky yourself*, she thought, and he did in an open-collared blue sport shirt, khakis, and running shoes.

"You said casual. This okay?" he asked, arms wide.

"You're perfect... I mean you're fine...yes, very casual," she sputtered as they walked out. *Get a grip, girl. We aren't even in the car!*

He held the door, and she slipped in, the soft leather seats of his Volvo SUV cool against her legs. His already familiar scent of spices and the sea filled the car, and she breathed deeply. *Relax, enjoy this,* she told herself as he came around and hopped in beside her.

~

"Great spot," he said, as Peggy, their waitress, set down drinks and disappeared.

"Yeah, it's nice," she said, sipping her cool crisp pinot grigio. She'd requested a window table, and they'd been given one of the best, a table at the restaurant's southeast corner with windows surrounding them on two sides.

"Thanks for coming. Much better than eating alone."

His eyes captured hers with an intensity that took her breath away. She gulped, willing her tone to nonchalance. "My pleasure." *Find a neutral safe topic*, she thought. "So, Barnum's Ledge? How did your day go?"

"Interesting." *But not as interesting as you.*

"Are you... Is your company going to make an offer?"

He nodded. "Tomorrow, but don't tell anyone. It'll be a process and a lot of back and forth, I'm guessing. We're still debating about demolition or restoration."

"I vote restoration."

"Me too, but not sure it's financially or structurally feasible after decades of deferred maintenance. Truth be told, I'd much rather talk about you."

Instantly, she turned red, her violet eyes registering surprise. "There's not much to tell. Married, divorced, one child, co-owner of a book business, still living at home, small-town girl at heart, I guess."

"So now you've told me the public version that I could've found out by asking around. I'm sure there's a lot more to you than that. I'm interested in the private Lolly Rogers, the one you don't let people see."

"Oh, here's Peggy to take our orders!" Lolly said, breathing a huge sigh of relief.

After Peggy left them, Lolly gazed up and met his eyes. "As you can see, I'm not very good at this. My evenings are usually spent with my mom, Maisie, or friends. Men, not so often."

Jack smiled, a warm, genuine smile that would melt an iceberg. He raised his glass. "Well, I hope you and I can be friends."

"Me too," she said, clinking her glass against his. "So tell me about you."

"Long divorced. Ex and I are friendly now, but it's taken a while. Kids are great."

"Divorce is tough, and it comes back to bite you when you least expect it. At least that's been my experience."

"Oh?"

"My ex just got remarried to Lucy's stepdaughter, Pam Morgan. I like Pam. I really do. It's just, adjusting to that new reality brings back the pain. Maybe I have trouble letting go?"

"I hear you."

"Now when Maisie stays with Sandy, she also has a new mommy."

"Well, you know that's not true. She's only ever going to have one mom."

"That's what Lucy says."

"She's right. Still sucks sometimes. About a year after my divorce, my ex and her new husband took Jack and Lyddie on a safari in Kenya. 'Bout ripped my heart out."

She looked up, surprised to see pain in his deep-blue eyes. "I'm sorry. It was bad enough when Sandy took Maisie to Disney last winter. I'm already steeling myself their family vacation this summer."

"It'll be weird going to Sandy's without Sandy at the helm," Lolly said.

"Can't wait for his next venture," Lucy said. "He and Richard have been talking about this idea of a farm-to-table restaurant near the winery."

Lolly shrugged. "Much tamer than the rock and roll life he's been used to. I suspect he could retire for life with what he got for the club, but somehow I don't see him in a Hawaiian shirt, Bermuda shorts, and sandals just yet."

"Once my husband gets an idea, he usually can't let it go. So if I had to guess, we'll be dining on great local food in a year or so."

"Maybe, now stop jabbering and let's get organized. Are Robert and his buddies all set to do the heavy lifting Thursday and Friday?"

Ice broken, they spent the rest of the meal with Jack describing his ideas for Barnum's Ledge and Lolly answering his questions about the village. After he paid the check, he said, "What do you think? Nightcap?"

"I shouldn't. I'm not a big drinker, and I don't want to be too late for Amy."

"I've got a better idea. Have you got an hour or so?"

"That's probably fine."

"It's a bright moonlit night. How about a ride out to Barnum's Ledge? I'd like to see it at night, and you can give me your ideas for its restoration."

CHAPTER 7

Jack sighed as they stood on the ledge, overlooking the bay. "So much more relaxing being here without Lindsay."

Lolly smiled. "Realtors are always a bit intense."

He chuckled. "I was going to say relentless, but that works. Mostly it's more relaxing because I'm not constantly on guard, ready to lunge over and catch her before she crashes over in those crazy shoes of hers."

Lolly laughed. "High heels have never been my friend."

"Good to know. Come on, shall we?" He turned toward the house. "It's perfectly safe. I have the key, and I know all the rotten spots."

They roamed through the rambling inn, rooms cobwebby and dark, the only light Jack's phone and a few overhead lights. As they ascended the stairs, he reached back and took her hand. "Probably safer this way."

His touch, firm and warm, sent shivers through her. It had been a long time since she'd held a man's hand. *Oh boy!*

When they reached the third-floor landing, he turned. "You okay?"

"Fine, as long as we're not going to fall three floors through rotting floorboards."

"It's pretty stable. I want to show you something." He led her forward to a door at the end of the hall, and they stepped into one of the inn's two tower rooms. "Cool, huh? It's my favorite part of the building."

"Very cool! I remember coming up here years ago. The view is spectacular."

They crossed the round room to gaze out the windows facing the water. Before them, a wide rippling moonlight path stretched across the bay, light dancing in tiny beams as far as one could see. "Beautiful," she said, just above a whisper.

"So are you," he said, his voice soft and gentle.

Lolly realized they were still holding hands, so she dropped his and took a step back. "What's happening here?"

"A man—me—is letting a beautiful woman—you—know that he finds you very attractive, and he's interested."

"Jack... I don't... I mean, I'm very flattered, but we don't know each other and I...well, I'm very out of practice."

"What if we plan to get to know each other better? Would that be such a bad thing?"

"I suppose not... I mean, of course not."

"Good. I won't pressure you, just friendly get-acquainted interactions? Shall we head down?" He offered his hand, and she took it.

As they descended in the semidarkness, she said, "Thanks for understanding. I feel like an awkward schoolgirl with her first crush."

"Crush. I like the sound of that. An auspicious start?"

She heard his chuckle even though she could barely see him. "Ha-ha, and watch where you're going. I may not be wearing heels, but I could still go flying."

"No worries milady. If you fall, I'll catch you."

Oh boy! Lolly thought.

Once outside, they strolled to the ledge to take one last look. As they stood gazing out at the water, he said, "Thanks for tonight. It was really great."

She turned to him, surprised by the soft cadence of his voice. "It was fun for me too."

"I'm going to go out on a limb here," he said, leaning in to kiss her softly.

Lolly closed her eyes and responded, sinking into his arms. Weak-kneed, she clung to him, his strong arms embracing her. Lost in a sea of sensation, she sighed as his tongue parted her lips, his kiss deepening. The howl of coyotes broke the silence, and she jumped back, shaking herself to regain her composure. *Friendly interactions indeed!*

Jack reached out to take her arm, steadying her. "You okay?"

"Yes...of course...it's late. I should...we should go." She turned and headed for the car.

"Lolly, wait!" he said, following her. She slipped into the car and shut the door as he approached.

He circled the SUV and got in. "You okay?"

Lolly looked straight ahead, afraid to meet his eyes. "Jack, I know I'm acting like a crazy person. You're a great guy, and I enjoy your company, I do. It's just...well, I don't know you, and this has happened very fast. This feels like more than friends, and I'm not sure how I feel about that."

"I agree. Let's get you home," he said softly.

When they reached the cottage, he hopped out and came around to open her door. "Better?" he asked, smiling.

Lolly sighed. "Yes. Are you still okay to drive Amy home?"

"Absolutely. Shall I wait here?"

"Of course not. Come in."

They found Amy watching television. "Everything go okay?" Lolly asked.

"Yup, she was a little angel. We had fun."

Lolly went to her purse and then handed Amy sixty dollars.

"This is too much," the pretty teenager said.

"Nonsense. It'll be spending money for out west. Jack's going to take you home, okay?"

Amy nodded, grabbing her backpack. He opened the door, and Lolly stepped onto the porch. "Thanks for taking her," she said.

"My pleasure." He leaned in to kiss her cheek. "Sleep well."

She reached up, touching her cheek that tingled in the aftermath of his kiss. Thinking back to her conversations with Lucy about finding a man, she smiled. *I've certainly found one, haven't I? And I don't have a clue what to do with him!* She waved as Jack backed up, then started down the drive.

CHAPTER 8

"Tell me something I can use," Jack said, gazing up from his notes to his foreman. They sat on the front porch of Barnum's Ledge, papers and maps spread out on two card tables. It was a warm morning, not a cloud in the sky, gulls circling the water in front of them. One swooped low, a spider crab in its beak as several others vied for its prize.

Pete Santoro scratched his head and met the razor-sharp eyes of his boss. "Depends." As Jack started to speak, Pete put up his hands. "Now hold on. What I mean is it depends on what you want. Do you want a spanking-new high-rise resort complex, or a cool, restored historic property? It'd be double or triple our usual costs if we ripped this sucker down and rebuilt a replica. Restoration won't be cheap, but nothing like that. We can at least keep the bones. One consideration, even when renovated, these old places are firetraps, so we'd probably want to put in firewall and nonflammable insulation like we did with Sojourner's Rest. That adds to cost." He referred to a resort they had completed several years earlier in southern Rhode Island.

"I'd like to keep the bones. Not sure what the big bosses will say, but let's assume that's what we're doing. Figure the cost, then I'll deal with Ms. Barnes. What about the outbuildings? Are they salvageable?"

"Some yes, some no. I suggest tearing down the barn and rebuilding. It's dangerous. All those lightning hits have taken a toll."

"Lightning rods get figured in for sure," Jack said, flipping through his folder of materials. "From all reports—not to mention the damage here—this place gets some major storms."

"We'll use air terminals like the Sojourner's," Pete said. "I also recommend tearing down the one-story kitchen addition and reworking the first floor. We could even blow something out the back."

"Yeah, you said that. Why?"

"The addition sits on the ledge. A major magnet for lightning even with the best equipment in the business."

Jack nodded. "Bumping out the back makes sense. Kitchen doesn't need the view, and I hate to take away from the first-floor spaces."

Pete grinned. "You've got a vision, then."

His boss chuckled, leaning back in his chair. "Something like that. I need a good architect, and I'd rather not use any on the Compass payroll. I'm going to do some scouting on the Q.T."

"So when's she coming by?"

"Two."

Pete's eyes widened. "Not much pressure, then."

"Do what you can. Rough is fine. Overestimate."

"Lemme get with Ray, and we'll see what we can come up with."

"Great. Let's meet up at the Café in town. Twelve thirty? Tell the guys I'll buy everyone lunch."

~

"We had fun, food was great. Period. End of story," Lolly said as the partners worked on plans for Friday's book fair. Over the last weeks of June, they held three book fairs in local schools focused on summer reading. Friday's was the high school fair.

"Define fun," Lucy said, giving her a mischievous look.

"Ha-ha. He's easy to talk to, has led an interesting life, and...he's a great kisser."

"Ooh—I knew it! I could see it the minute you walked in."

"One kiss, probably a mistake, but yes, it was..." *What was it? Magical, that's what.* "Nice... It was a nice kiss."

"Nice? What kind of description is that? When did it happen? How long did it last?"

"Barnum's Ledge, a minute or two. And that's all I'm going to say. We have so much work to do."

"Party pooper," Lucy said, making notes as she packed books in several boxes near the door. "I see lots of promise here, and that's good. Can't wait for Friday night!"

"So you guys are coming?"

"You know Richard. He loves to support local talent, and he actually likes the Cherry Pickers," Lucy said, referring to Lolly's sister Marla's band. The group's mix of country, bluegrass, and jazz, and a few rock and roll hits appealed to a wide audience, so they usually drew a big crowd.

"It'll be weird going to Sandy's without Sandy at the helm," Lolly said.

"What's he going to do now anyway?" Lucy asked.

"I suspect he could retire for life with what he got for the club, but I don't see him in a Hawaiian shirt, Bermuda shorts, and sandals just yet. If you remember, he had to sign an agreement not to open another music venue within fifty miles."

"He told Richard he's considering small-scale building projects. Maybe he'll become some sort of high-end flipper?"

"Hmm...not my business, now stop jabbering and let me get organized. Are Robert and his buddies all set to do the heavy lifting Thursday and Friday?"

"They are," Lucy said, referring to her twenty-year-old son.

Lolly gave her a thumbs-up. "Then let's get cracking!" *So I can stop thinking about Jack Faulkner and his dreamy blue eyes.*

~

"ALL OUT OF SCHOOL?" LOLLY ASKED HARRIET, LUCY'S SISTER, WHO they had met for lunch at the Café.

"Yup. Just got to do report cards, and I'm ready for summer." Harriet taught at a private Quaker school, Hampton Friends, in a town just north of Horseshoe Crab Cove.

"Oh, boy," Lucy said, eyes on the café's front door. "Guess who just walked in."

Lolly turned in time to spy Jack as he closed the door and gazed around, clearly looking for someone. "Oh, geez." Her spine tingled, and her insides turned to mush. "Maybe he won't see us."

No such luck. His eyes found hers, and he waved, heading across the crowded space. "Hey, ladies!" he said once he reached them.

"Hey, yourself," Lucy said. "Nice to see you again. Jack, this is my sister Harriet."

Harriet reached out and shook his hand.

"Nice to meet you, Ms....?"

"Morgan, but please call me Harriet."

"There sure are a lot of Morgans around here," he said. "Met your village vet this morning when my guys and I were eating breakfast."

Harriet smiled. "Kyle's my husband."

"And my husband's nephew," Lucy added.

"Small world. I've actually been trying to reach Westcott Associates, an architectural firm in Maryland, because I want to fly one of their architects up here to look at Barnum's Ledge. His name is Morgan too."

"Sam Morgan?" Harriet asked.

"The very one. Do you know him?"

Harriet laughed. "My brother-in-law."

"And also my husband's nephew," Lucy said.

Jack shook his head, a wide grin on his handsome face. "All roads lead to Morgan?"

"Something like that," Lucy said. "What led you to Sam?"

"What didn't? The guy's written up every other month in the trade journals. One of the country's up-and-comers."

"He's very talented," Harriet said, "and not just because he's my brother-in-law."

Lucy nodded. "Richard brought his Maine crew down for the farm, but had Sam draw up the plans for the winery."

Lolly had remained silent, watching them converse, so she was caught off guard when Jack turned to her. "How are you?"

"Fine...great...couldn't be better," she sputtered.

His grin widened as he eyed the doorway where four men had entered. With a private nod to her, he turned to the sisters. "A pleasure ladies. My crew's here, so I've got to scoot. I look forward to seeing you all Friday, if not before." With that, he made his way back through the room.

"Wow, what a cutie. Where'd he come from?" Harriet asked, observing Jack's retreat.

"Boston," Lolly replied.

"And he's staying next door to my partner here," Lucy said. "They've gotten real friendly since his arrival."

Harriet's eyes widened. "Oh? Tell me more!"

CHAPTER 9

A cool evening breeze wafted across the fields as Jack leaned back on the comfortable glider on the cottage's back porch. The soft canvas felt slightly damp after a late-afternoon shower, but the coolness felt good after the heat of the day and a long negotiating session with Lindsay. He'd grabbed a sandwich on his way through town, but his dinner lay half eaten on the table beside him.

Maybe it was time to do something else?

For many years, he'd loved the wrangling, the wheeling and dealing, the thrill of the chase, but now it felt old and stale. Sitting across the table from yet another cute suit ready and willing to flirt and anything else necessary to make a sale no longer thrilled him. It felt sad and pointless. He'd seen too many Lindsay Barneses over the years, and he'd had enough. Not that he succumbed to the Realtor's charms and propositions—never—but it was all a game, a back-and-forth dance that went on and on until there was a winner. He usually won, as he had today. Lindsay had taken Compass's offer and promised to let him know by the weekend. As he rose to leave her office, she said, "No promises. This isn't what they expected. Not even close," but he was relatively certain that the offer, along with pages of notes, photos, and repair estimates, would ultimately prevail. There might be a slight protest, but he'd win in the end.

He closed his eyes and was drifting off when his cell buzzed and Marsha's name appeared. "Shit," he muttered as he clicked on. "Marsha, hey."

"Where are you?" *No hello, no how are you?*

"I'm away. On business. What's up?"

"What's up? My surgery's next week, Poppy's gone off the deep end again, and I've had to hire private detectives to try to find her."

One step at a time, he told himself, counting slowly to ten before replying. "It's a face lift, which you elected to do. If you're stressed, why not put it off?"

"Put it off? Do you have any idea how long it takes to get into that practice? I've been waiting over a year."

Don't I know it, Jack thought. It had been her main topic of conversation before their split four months earlier. "I'm sorry to hear about Poppy." Marsha's seventeen-year-old had been in and out of rehab as long as he'd known her. A gifted soccer player, she'd become addicted to prescription drugs after an injury and had really never pulled out of it. In and out of school, she would disappear for weeks, then show up, beg for one more chance, complete rehab, return to school, then the cycle would repeat itself. Jack hadn't seen Poppy since he and her mother broke up.

"She's pregnant."

"Geez, with who?"

"Could have been any number of her loser boyfriends."

"Is Chuck helping you?" he asked, referring to Marsha's ex-husband, one of the city's most respected pulmonologists.

"Yes, he's opened his wallet. He always does. As for the rest, you can forget it."

"Again, I'm sorry," he said, gritting his teeth, refusing to get sucked back into the drama. It had taken several months before the final break to extricate himself from life with Marsha, and he refused to get pulled back in.

"I need you, Jack."

"Not this time."

"I made a mistake. One mistake, and I've said I'm sorry a million times."

He doubted her affair with a fellow attorney in her office had been the first, but had no wish to get into a discussion about her infidelities or anything about a relationship that had been a mistake from the start. "Marsha, we're not together. It's over, and that's not going to change. I'm sorry for what you're going through with Poppy. I hope you find her soon and—"

"Bastard, why do I bother!"

The phone clicked off, and he let out a sigh. *Must screen your calls, buddy.*

Restless, he stood. There was still a good hour of daylight, so he laced his running shoes and headed toward the beach path. Maybe if it was low tide, he'd even try a run. He could smell the sea before he emerged from the path onto the cliffs, the salt air clearing his head as he left behind Marsha's phone call and the afternoon with Lindsay. Low tide below, the beach was empty with at least a half mile of relatively sandy ground. He descended and broke into a gentle jog, his usual pace these days. The river was calm, waves lapping the shore and the cries of gulls the only sounds. At the end of the open space, he turned and headed back, slowing to walking when halfway back. It was then that he heard voices and laughter and gazed up, spying Maisie and her mother skipping down the path from Netherfield Manor.

It was clear they hadn't seen him, so he headed their way, meeting them as the child danced onto the sand. "Hey, Maisie! Lolly."

"Hi, Jack! Mommy and I came from Grandma's."

"Good dinner?"

"The best! Where did you eat?"

"My nice little cottage where I guarantee my dinner wasn't as good as yours." He gazed up at Lolly. "Hey."

"Hey."

"How's your day been?"

"Busy. Yours?" He looked tired, his eyes troubled. Not at all like the man who'd taken her to dinner.

He managed a smile. "I've had better."

"We all have those days. Maisie and I are crab hunting. Want to join us?"

"I'd love to."

They spent the next half hour turning over rocks and boulders, Maisie squealing as small green crabs skittered everywhere. They waded into the shallows and found horseshoe crabs, starfish, and whelks, all of which were examined and let go. As they headed up the path toward home, the adults followed Maisie.

Jack turned to her. "Thanks. I really needed this."

She smiled, at ease and comfortable. "You looked as if you'd lost your best friend back there."

"Lot of stuff going on."

Impulsively, she reached out and touched his arm. "I'm actually a pretty good listener. Not tonight, of course, with my little buddy in tow."

"Thanks, that's kind. My shit. I'll deal with it. No sense in burdening anyone else." His voice had a hard edge she hadn't heard in their previous encounters.

"Well, this is you," she said when they reached his cottage's lawn. "Night."

"Night," he said, waving to the child who was already half-hidden in the path to their cottage.

"Here's a thought," she said, surprised at her sudden boldness. "Why don't you have dinner with Maisie and me tomorrow night? That is, if you're not busy? Something simple. As you saw, we don't live in Netherfield Manor."

"I'd love to. What can I bring?"

"Yourself."

"What time?"

"Six?"

"Perfect. See you then, if not around town tomorrow."

Stunned, Lolly walked across the lawn. *What have I done? Invited a neighbor to dinner, a neighbor who looks like he needs a friend. That's it. End of story! Yeah right, and I'm Cinderella!*

CHAPTER 10

"That was amazing," Jack said, gazing from mother to child.

"I stirred the sauce!" Maisie said, waving her fork, which held several strands of pasta.

Lolly smiled, reaching over to tame the fork. "There's more." She'd made what she called a low-fat version of pasta carbonara and a colorful salad with lettuces, tomatoes, and cucumbers from their greenhouse. She and Jack were enjoying a crisp sauvignon blanc he'd brought, while Maisie had water in her water bottle.

"Thanks, but I'm stuffed. This is a beautiful home." He gazed around the cozy dining room open to the adjacent living room. "Who's the artist?" he asked, indicating several soft impressionist-style landscapes on the walls. They appeared to be local scenes.

"Mommy did 'em!" Maisie said. "We paint all the time. I'll go get one of mine!" The child hopped up and disappeared.

"Wow! They're really lovely." *As are you*, he thought, smiling at her. Dressed casually in a vee-necked T-shirt and jeans, she wore her hair tied back in a ponytail, tendrils falling around her face. *Beautiful.*

Lolly blushed, the intensity of his gaze unnerving. "Thanks, but it's just a hobby."

"I like to paint too. Watercolors. Strictly amateur. Took a few classes years ago. Part of my moving on strategy post-divorce."

Lolly laughed. "Something we have in common. I took a bunch of painting classes through the Newport Art Museum as part of my get-a-life campaign."

"Did it work?"

She waved her hand. "You tell me."

He grinned. "The paintings are incredible. I meant the get-a-life part."

She shrugged. "That's still a work in progress. Uh-oh... Maisie, did you take all those down?"

"Yup!" she said, a pile of frames in her arms. Without further ado, she pushed Jack's plate out of the way and set the frames one by one in front of him. Images of animals in vibrant primary hues, they had been matted and framed by someone with an eye for color.

"These are awesome!" he said. "Totally awesome."

Maisie beamed. "Mommy and Grandma framed them."

Lolly rose and began clearing. "Maise, why don't you show Jack where they go, and he can help you rehang them?"

After dinner, they played several games of Go Fish before Lolly announced, "Time for bed."

"Better if I head out?" he asked.

"Up to you. Bedtime routine with stories and washing up takes about a half hour. If you'd like to hang around, I can make coffee, or a nightcap? Your choice."

Oh, I will definitely be hanging around. "You go ahead. I'll wash up from dinner, then enjoy your back porch. That's my favorite thing about my cottage. I love a screened-in porch."

She smiled. "Me too. Thanks. Maisie, say good night to Jack."

In answer, her daughter flung herself into his arms hugging him tightly. "Night, Jack!"

Surprised, he returned her hug. "Thanks for having me. See you soon!"

～

"All settled in?" he asked as Lolly joined him on the porch. Her scent of honeysuckle and lemon mingled with the gentle evening breeze.

"Conked out. It was a busy day. Can I get you something? Coffee? A drink? I usually have seltzer at this time of night. Not very exciting."

"Seltzer sounds great."

Before she departed, she lit two lanterns, their candles throwing soft light in the growing darkness. Several minutes later, she returned. "Cans okay? They stay colder that way."

"Perfect, thanks," he said, reaching up to take the can of cranberry-lime seltzer. He patted the seat beside him on the wide porch glider, similar to the one at his cottage, but much more comfortable.

She'd intended to take one of the chairs opposite him, but came around and sat at the opposite end of the glider.

"Love these things," he said, giving a gentle push of his foot.

"Yeah, they're nice. Mom found a bunch of them at an antique place when she was decorating the cottages."

"Lucky you."

"So tell me something about you. Thanks to Mother and the village grapevine, you probably know all you need to know about me."

He chuckled. "Hardly. My life's had its ups and downs like everyone else's. Married right out of college. Cynthia and I kind of grew up together, then grew apart. We're still friendly, but she was a little too friendly with a bunch of men during the marriage."

"Join the club. Where does she live now?"

"Maine. Her family has kind of a compound up there."

"Oh, that's right. On the island?"

"They have the summer houses on the island. The compound is farther south, on the coast off Kennebunkport. "

"Bush territory. Fancy. I've heard of those places."

He leaned back grinning widely. "Hate to break it to you, but you're living in one."

"I suppose I am, but it sounds much cooler if it's in Maine."

"It was cool. Is cool. The island too," he said, leaning back, his voice wistful.

"So how many years have you been single?"

"It's been almost ten years since the divorce."

"That's not exactly what I asked."

He chuckled. "Yeah, I've dated and had a thing for almost two years with a woman."

Lolly sat up, turning to him. "Thing?"

"We lived together. Officially ended when I moved out four months ago. It was really over much earlier. Kind of a mess, really."

His brow furrowed, and in the lantern light, she glimpsed pain in his eyes. "You know what? Enough about the past. Let's hear more about your plans for Barnum's Ledge."

"We don't have it yet. I'd rather not jinx it, *and* I'd much rather talk about you and your beautiful Liz Taylor eyes," he said softly, his hand reaching over to brush errant strands of hair from her forehead, tracing a line to her cheek.

"You can thank my mother for these."

"Thank you, Mavis! So how are you still single?" His fingers lingered on her cheek, caressing gently.

"Honest answer? I'm a basket case. I've spent years angry at my ex when I was the one who drove him away. He was absolutely justified in seeking the companionship and love of others. I was only a wife to him for about a minute."

"Not compatible?"

"Probably. On top of that, I suffered major postpartum depression after Maisie was born. I wouldn't let anyone near me."

He nodded. "Cynthia had some of that after Jack Junior's birth."

"It was awful. Went on for over a year. By then, I'd driven Sandy away and was living above Lucy's garage. Thank goodness Mother bought her estate so Maisie and I had a place to live. Lucy saved my life when we started the business together."

"Sorry you had that dark time."

"We really are getting way too maudlin. No more past!" she said, sitting up straight and reaching for her seltzer.

"I couldn't agree more," he said, taking her hand. "To the present," he added, leaning in, his lips finding hers.

Lolly responded, the kiss deepening with lots of tongue and sighs of pleasure. Her arms circled his shoulders as he drew her closer, his strong chest against her, hands moving up to cup her breasts. "Lovely," he murmured, teasing her nipples to ripeness through her T-shirt and bra.

She sighed, arching into his embrace, her fingers running through his thick hair, caressing, stroking. She broke the kiss as his lips moved down her neck. "I haven't done this in a *really* long time," she whispered.

"Good. That way you'll have forgotten how it's done in case I fumble." Deftly, he lifted her, bringing her to straddle his lap, his hands under her T-shirt now, nudging her lacy bra aside to caress her glorious full breasts.

"Oh, oh," she said, lost in a sea of sensation. Suddenly they heard a sound from inside the house. "Oh, shit," she whispered. "Maisie."

Lolly hopped up, adjusting her top. "Hey, honey, is that you?" she called as a tiny figure appeared at the door.

"I heard something," Maisie said, rubbing her eyes, voice sleepy.

"Probably just the wind, sweetie."

"I'm scared."

Lolly went to the door and picked her up. "Come on, sweet girl. Back to bed." She turned back to Jack. "I'm sorry. This might take a while."

Grinning, he stood. "I'm gonna go and let you girls get some sleep."

Lolly gave him a rueful smile. "Probably best. Say good night to Jack, Maisie."

"Night," a tiny voice said, muffled against her mother's shoulder.

Lolly gazed over at him, mouthing *sorry*.

"No problem. What time can I pick you up Friday night?"

"Seven?"

"Perfect. See you then, if not before."

As Lolly sang to Maisie, her favorite song, "Baby Beluga," she thought about the evening. *It's been too long.* She sighed, remembering the touch of his magic hands.

A small voice interrupted her musings. "Mommy?"

"Yes, baby?"

"I thought I was at Daddy's."

She kissed her round forehead, damp with sweat. "You were dreaming, baby."

Maisie shook her head. "No, it was the same sounds...you know, Dad and Pammy. It sounded like them and the noises they make in their bedroom."

Oh geez, shoot me now. "A dream, baby. That's all it was." She didn't know whether to laugh or cry.

CHAPTER 11

"Oh my God, it was incredible," Lolly said as the partners carried boxes down the back stairs to one of the farm trucks. They were headed for the regional high school to set up tomorrow's book fair.

"I'm glad," Lucy said, smiling at her.

"But how can I have a relationship with a seven-year-old in the house?"

"Well, there are all the nights Maisie spends with her dad. Those are possibilities."

"He's also leaving town in a few weeks."

"Who knows?" Lucy said in a singsong voice.

"I know," she said, plunking the last box on the truck bed. "Tell me again why we didn't get Rob and his buddies to help on this end?"

"They're meeting us over there with the hand truck."

"You didn't answer my question."

"He's works for his father Thursday mornings."

"No excuse. Let's pick up sandwiches before we head over."

∼

AT ONE O'CLOCK THURSDAY, JACK HEADED TOWARD BARNUM'S LEDGE to meet Lindsay. Anticipating the fight ahead, he'd spent the morning on the phone with his bosses. As he parked, his cell rang and he spied "Marsha" on the caller ID. He set the phone to vibrate and didn't answer. *I'll have to take care of that*, he thought, grabbing his briefcase and waving to Lindsay, who stood next to her car, cell phone to her ear.

"Gotta go, ciao," she said, clicking off and slipping the phone into her purse. "Hi, Jack!"

They sat at the makeshift table Jack had asked his men to set up on the porch. The bay sparkled on this glorious June day, providing a spectacular backdrop for the meeting. Dressed to impress as always, the Realtor wore a sleeveless gray linen dress and matching jacket, removing the latter to drape it over the back of her chair. Not a hair out of place, she wore lapis earrings and a matching necklace, a dozen bangle bracelets on her right arm. When she noticed him looking at her arm, she twirled it. "My Alex and Ani collection. I'm addicted, I'm afraid."

He smiled, but didn't remark on either her jewels or appearance. *No sense feeding the fire.* Marsha had loved that same brand and always provided him with a long wish list on birthdays and holidays. He found them rather tacky, but dutifully sought out each trinket to please her. After several minutes of shuffling papers, he began. "So, where do we stand?"

"The Barnums have considered your offer. They feel it is woefully under what the property is worth, but because they like your plans for the inn, they've made a counteroffer."

After Lindsay presented their unrealistic counteroffer, he wanted to laugh, but instead held his tongue, gazed out at the bay and took several deep breaths. Finally when he turned back, he was smiling. "Just when I was getting to like it here. I guess my work is done." He began shoving papers back into his briefcase.

"But...but... Jack, this is only the beginning," she sputtered. "I mean...I told the family...we would discuss and go back and forth."

"What's the point?" he asked.

"I mean…they are very eager to sell."

"Good luck to them at that price. It's a pretty little village, but it's not Nantucket or Newport or Block Island. The inn's got a great location, which is why we offered what we did, but it's a tear-down, even if someone decides to restore it."

Not quite successful in hiding her dismay, she whined, "It's the sentimental value. So many of the Barnums spent childhood summers here."

"And they can in future if the property is restored. Hell, we'd even have thrown in a few weeks' lodging—a room or two set aside for Barnum family members each summer."

"Really?"

"That's pretty standard practice when Compass buys a family estate."

"Well, I could ask. Any wiggle room on the price?"

"Nope. And I'll need to know by the end of the weekend. I've got another property up the coast to evaluate if this falls through."

"I'll bring it to them today. I suppose dinner tonight is out?"

"Sorry, I've got to go to Boston for the night."

"Leaving us already?"

"The Barnums will decide that for me."

"I was hoping to catch a glimpse of our dreamy Jack," Mavis said as she sat down to dinner with her daughter and granddaughter.

"He's not home," Maisie said, grabbing a warm roll from the basket.

"Only one, Maise, or you'll spoil your dinner." Lolly had repeatedly asked that her mother not serve dinner rolls, which she never touched but felt should be on every well-appointed dinner menu. Kendall usually ended up donating them to the local food bank or giving them to Maisie to feed to the ducks.

"Yes, I know, precious. He phoned this afternoon. Had to go back to Boston."

Lolly's heart sank. She'd planned to walk the back way home behind his cottage, hoping to catch a glimpse of him. *What did I expect? No reason for him to phone*, she mused, nodding as Kendall set her plate of fresh pasta and summer vegetables in front of her.

"What's that long face about?" her mother asked.

"Long day, that's all. Book fair tomorrow."

"What's my baby doing while you're involved with that?"

"I'm a helper!" Maisie said, sitting up, chin jutted out. "I'm the bagger."

Mavis frowned, violet eyes turned on her daughter. "Is that a good idea?"

"Does it all the time. She's the best helper in the world."

"But it's a very long day."

"Daddy's picking me up at lunchtime!"

"Well, that's a relief," Mavis said, waving away the sauce Kendall offered. "What's Daddy doing these days now that he no longer owns the club?"

"I thought you'd have heard," Lolly said, grabbing a piece of bread to soak up the garlicky sauce. "He and Pam's dad are going into business together."

Eyes big as saucers, Mavis set down her fork. "What?"

"Farm-to-table restaurant. They're clearing land now on the north end of Morgan's Fire. Gonna be cool. It's apparently modeled on a place they loved out west."

Mavis rolled her eyes. "Isn't everything around here these days? I swear that Arizona crowd has turned this place upside down."

"In good ways. They can serve local produce from Land's End, and apparently, Richard Morgan's considering raising beef, pigs, and chickens."

"Well, I never! That man is insatiable."

Lolly chuckled. "He likes to keep busy, according to Lucy."

"I should say so." Mavis turned to her granddaughter. "What do you think of all this, precious?"

"I like chickens and pigs!"

"Not when they wind up on your dinner plate."

"Mother!"

"Daddy says I can have my own pig and some chickens."

"Where will you keep them?"

"At the farm. He's also gonna let me take riding lessons."

Mavis frowned, gazing at Lolly. "Not at Land's End?"

Lolly shook her head. "Since Weezie Morgan started her pony camps, they're not doing pony camps or kids' lessons these days, Karen told me. Just their old regulars."

"Mark my words. She'll be moving out there too once she marries Rich Morgan," Mavis said, referring to Karen Miller, her neighbor's daughter. Faith Miller, Karen's mother, was a fellow Darn Yarner, one of the group of eight women friends in the village that included Mavis, Lucy's mom, Helen, and others.

"Maybe. Or maybe they'll decide to live on Land's End? Or somewhere completely different?"

"Humph," Mavis said, waving to Kendall to clear the plates. "Let's have ice cream for dessert tonight. What do you say, Maisie-bean?"

"Yes!"

CHAPTER 12

"Please, Jack. All I'm asking is that you talk to her. She listens to you."

Jack sat in the company condo on the city's waterfront, two blocks from Faneuil Hall. Marsha sat across the room perched on one of the bar stools, sipping a diet soda to which she'd helped herself out of the company minibar. He could feel a migraine building. Marsha's voice was like the screech of nails on a chalkboard. "It's not my place to speak to Poppy. Never was, but especially now. I'm not her father, and it sounds like she needs him." A mental image of eight months earlier flashed through his mind, when they had returned home to find Poppy ripping their flat-screen television from the living room wall.

"Well, that's not happening. As you well know, Chuck is worse than useless. Poppy loves you, not him."

"Marsha, we've had this conversation a million times. Poppy never gave a shit about me or what I said, and you know it. The only relationship we had was monetary—me bailing her out of one mess after another."

Her eyes narrowed, and her expression hardened. "I never realized how selfish you are."

"If you want to call it that, fine. Excuse me." He stood and headed for the bathroom to get his headache medication. When he returned, she'd moved to the sofa and was patting the seat beside her.

He grabbed a bottle of water from the fridge and sat in a chair opposite the sofa.

"Spoilsport," she said, coyly batting her eyelashes.

"Marsha, this really does have to stop. We're done. Let's not pretend we aren't. Now I'm in the middle of a job, so I have to get back. Sometime soon, you and I need to work out what do to about the condo. Have you decided if you want to stay?"

"I can't afford it on my own, as you well know."

"Then we sell? Should I contact Murray? Is it ready to be shown?"

"Hardly."

"Well then, just let me know when it is."

"Fees are due."

Jack paid the mortgage, and Marsha had handled the condo fees. "And?"

"Since you walked out on me, I should think the least you can do is pay the monthly fee. There's an assessment too, for the new walkways. Two thousand."

"When's it due?"

"By the end of July."

"Fine. I'll take care of it." *Anything to get her off my back.*

"How about dinner tonight?"

"Can't. I'm eating with Roland," he said, referring to his boss.

"Then lunch tomorrow?"

"I don't think so. I've got to head back to the jobsite."

She leaned forward, her off-white vee-neck sweater affording a bird's-eye view of her anorexic chest and almost nonexistent cleavage. "Which is where?"

Marsha was the polar opposite of Lolly, her skeletal frame all sharp angles. Her shoulder-length auburn hair framed an oval face, unnaturally shiny and plump from recent Botox injections and cheek implants. Faint scars from several plastic surgeries crisscrossed her forehead, chin, and neck.

"Little village. You won't have heard of it." *Was she really this ugly when we were together?* he thought. It wasn't so much her looks, but her demeanor. There was a clawing nastiness to Marsha that hadn't surfaced right away, or he'd been too blinded by the sex to notice.

"Try me."

"Bayport," he said, not really sure why he lied.

"That's not so little. What kind of property?"

"A resort."

"In Bayport? Who the hell would want to go to that shithole?"

"Listen, Marsha, I've got work to do before I head over to Roland's."

"Can you please help with Poppy? I know you think she doesn't listen, but she does. If I find her by tomorrow, can you just stop in before you head back to Hicksville?"

Tired of arguing, he nodded. "Fine, but I need to get on the road by early afternoon."

Marsha stood, leaving her glass on the coffee table. Grabbing her purse from the counter, she sidled back, bent over, and kissed his cheek. "Thanks sweetie. See you tomorrow."

"Maybe. I may only be able to manage a phone call."

"We'll see," she said, sashaying to the door, waving over her shoulder. "Toodle-oo!"

"We'll see" is right, he thought, leaning back and closing his eyes.

He wondered if he should go back to the cottage after dinner with his boss. That way, he'd be out of range and could speak to Poppy by phone. As it was, the choice was made for him.

CHAPTER 13

Lolly gazed around the gymnasium, pleased at the crowd they'd attracted. Focused on summer reading, the tables displayed the titles required for high school students well as beach reads for adolescents and adults. She caught her partner's eye and gave her a thumbs-up just as a voice spoke from behind her.

"Great turnout," he said, as Lolly turned to find her ex-husband.

She gazed up at the man who still gave off a smoldering heat that was hard to ignore. His coal-black eyes danced with warmth, and his thick, dark hair was tied back in a ponytail. *That's a new look*, she thought. "Hey," she said. "She's been waiting for you.

Sandy stooped to hug Maisie. "Hey sweet pea."

"Hi, Daddy! "I'm ready."

"Great." He turned to Lolly. "Pam's working. We're meeting her in town for lunch. Want us to pick something up for you and Lucy?"

"Thanks, but Richard's bringing food soon."

Maisie tugged at his belt. "There's my friend Chelsea. Can I go see her?"

"Sure, kiddo. Just stay where I can see you." As their daughter ran off, he turned to Lolly. "Got any good mysteries to recommend?"

She gave him a look, then pointed. "On the tables under the hoop. There's a pretty good selection."

"How've you been?"

"Fine. Same ole, same ole. Working, trying to stay sane living under Mother's roof."

"You look good."

"Thanks, you too." *But then you always do.*

"You've probably heard from Lucy about the restaurant?"

She smiled, raising an eyebrow. "I have. A little tame for you after all that rock and roll, isn't it?"

"Maybe, but I like the idea of farm-to-table. We all loved Vermillion, that restaurant in Saguaro Valley."

"So I heard. I'd love to see that place. The Valley, I mean. Sounds amazing."

"It's pretty cool, but I'll take ocean anytime. We're scouting locations on the farm and think we're found a perfect spot on the bluffs near the winery."

"Lucky you. Will Pam be involved?"

"Not much. It's not her thing. We're not rushing either, 'cause I want Murph to come on board, and he's committed to helping Liz Cady get the lay of the land out at Sandy's."

"Oh?" she asked.

"Yup, Cady Promotions has hired him for an exorbitant salary. He's giving her two months. There's a good chance she'll buy him and keep him, but right now, he's insisting he wants to come back to work for me. Time will tell."

"If the rumors about what Elizabeth Cady paid for Sandy's are true, you can certainly match her salary."

He shrugged. "We'll see. Well, I'd better check out those mysteries and corral our rug rat."

Lolly rolled her eyes. "Don't call her that. Check out John Sandford. He's really popular right now and I think you'd like him since you love Harlan Coban. There's also the latest Michael Connelly."

"I notice you didn't recommend any women writers."

"Ha-ha. Look where that got me with all your obnoxious comments about Sara Paretsky and Louise Penny."

"Hey, I liked those ladies. Just didn't relate."

Lolly waved her arms, shooing him off. "On your way. Your daughter's getting antsy."

She sighed, watching him head for the mysteries. *Why do we get along so well now, but couldn't manage a civil word during our marriage?*

"Hey, partner, penny for your thoughts," Lucy said, coming to stand beside her.

"Who's manning the register?"

"Lynn, as you can see." Lucy inclined her head toward Lynn Casey, who worked part-time for Merlin's Closet. "You okay? I see you-know-who is here."

"Fine. I'm fine, really. In fact, I was just wondering why we get along so well now and we didn't back then."

"Different times?" Lucy smiled, a mischievous expression playing in her eyes. "And maybe a certain gorgeous neighbor of yours?"

"Ha-ha. Just got a voicemail. He can't make it tonight."

"Why?"

"Has to stay in Boston. Some personal issue. He didn't elaborate."

"Well then, Richard and I will pick you up."

Lolly leaned on her shoulder. "Thanks, partner."

"Oh, almost forgot why I came over. Lunch is in the room next door. Callie sent a basket of sandwiches and stuff," Lucy said, referring to their housekeeper and cook.

"Great, I'll grab something in a while," Lolly said, as she observed Sandy with Maisie in one arm, a big stack of books in the other.

After paying, he looked back and gave her a wave as they headed for the exit. She gazed over at Richard and Lucy, his arm draped casually on her shoulder as she recommended books to customers. *Men,* she mused. *Will I ever get lucky like Lucy?*

CHAPTER 14

Jack sat with his boss at Tops, a popular bar not far from the office, enjoying an after-dinner brandy. A true mentor, Roland Jenkins was one of the steadiest men he knew. A silver fox with thick gray hair and piercing gray eyes, he'd been married to the same woman for forty-two years. "So tell me more about this property," Jenkins said, leaning back and taking a sip of his drink. "Sounds more personal to you."

Jack grinned. "Maybe. Brings out my latent dreams of being an old-fashioned innkeeper, I guess."

"Inn or resort? Compass doesn't do inns."

"Maybe we should."

His boss raised an eyebrow. "What's going on, buddy?"

"Nothing, everything. Messy breakup with Marsha still ongoing, and her daughter's a nightmare. Hard to disengage, you know?" Roland had been witness to some of the drama of Marsha and family. In fact, they'd taken several trips together as couples, so his boss knew Marsha pretty well.

"Never liked the woman. Reminds me of a skinny vulture."

Jack laughed. "Now you tell me."

"Well, you were smitten. What could I have said?"

"You're right. My problem."

"But that's not what's going on here. I know you, Faulkner. There's something or someone down there in Horseshoe Crab Cove, isn't there?"

"Maybe... She's actually pretty terrific, but I'm not about to get involved until all this is sorted out."

"Looks like you already are."

He shrugged. "Story of my life."

The men parted company in the parking lot. "Good luck down there," Roland said. "And remember—resort, not inn, or Compass isn't interested."

Jack nodded. As he headed to his car, his cell phone buzzed with an unfamiliar number. He clicked on. "Hello?'

"Mr. Faulkner?"

"Yes, who's calling?"

"This is Lynn Fallon. I'm a nurse in the emergency room at Salem Hospital. We have a Poppy Blake here, and she's asked for you."

"Jesus," Jack muttered, noting the address. "I'll be there as soon as I can."

Sandy's was hopping, Marla LaSalle's band, the Cherry Pickers, in fine form as dancers crowded the floor. Lolly twirled around the floor, laughing as she danced between her business partner and Lucy's sister Harriet. During slow dances, of which there were few, Richard and Kyle Morgan stepped out to dance with their wives. Otherwise, they seemed content at the bar. As the band began "I Need You," Lolly headed off the floor and bumped into Kevin Averill. "Hey, Lolly, wanna dance?"

"Hi, Kev," she said, extending her hand. She'd always had a soft spot for the son of Hank Averill, owner of Averill's General Store. Her sister's high school classmate, he was a gentle giant, with scruffy brown hair and soft green eyes. Labeled as "a bit slow," Kevin did odd jobs around the village when not working at his father's store. As he was strong as an ox, Lucy and Lolly often hired him to work the book fairs, loading and unloading boxes as he had that day. Only a few hours earlier, Kevin and his battered truck had hauled the boxes of unsold books back to the barn at Morgan's Fire and carefully stacked them along the wall.

Clumsy at times, Kevin was a surprisingly good dancer. As they moved to the music, they chatted about the day, and she thanked him again for all his help. The song was winding down when he said, "Marla looks real pretty tonight."

"Always does. She got the good genes." She followed his gaze to her sister, who was singing the romantic duet with her on-again off-again boyfriend, Richie. From the looks of it, they were on this week. Lolly didn't much care for Richie and thought he treated her sister like shit, but she stayed out of Marla's affairs as much as possible, since their mother harped enough for ten people. Kevin had had a crush on Marla as long as Lolly could remember, poor guy. The longing in his eyes made her sad.

As the song ended, the band started playing another Tim McGraw tune, "I Like It, I Love It," and before she knew what was happening, they were flying around the dance floor again. For a big man, he could move!

When she finally sat down, laughing and exhausted several dances later, she pulled out her cell phone. No calls. *Another dead end,* she mused, wondering if it was time to go home. Lucy and Harriet appeared, sitting on either side of her.

"Wow, you were swinging!" Harriet said, smiling at her.

"All Kevin," Lolly said. "And I'm beat. Should I look around for another party pooper to take me home? I don't want to spoil your fun."

"Kyle and I are leaving soon. He's got early rounds tomorrow," she said. "And his brother Sam's coming in for a night or two."

"Really, that's great."

Harriet nodded. "Jack managed to coax him up to look at Barnum's Ledge."

"Richard's got him roped into the restaurant too," Lucy said.

"With his reputation, they'd be lucky to get him, but what about

Richard's usual guys? They've been with him forever, right? Won't they have their noses out of joint if he doesn't use them?" Lolly asked.

Lucy smiled. "Family trumps business. Besides, Morgan Enterprises gives them plenty of business. They're doing some huge project in Singapore with them right now."

"A different universe." Lolly smiled at Harriet. "I'd really like to find a ride home before midnight."

"Richard would probably be fine with leaving, so we can take you too," Lucy said.

Lolly looked from one sister to the other. "Both your husbands look very happy at the bar. Let's wait until one of them comes this way and hints to go home."

"That could be a while," Lucy said. "Once Richard finds a kindred spirit, he's lost to me."

Her handsome husband leaned against the long bar, chatting with Kyle, Sandy Rodriquez, and several other men, including Murph O'Neill, the interim manager of the club.

"Where's Pam anyway?" Lolly asked.

"She and Elise went to a play in Bayport," Lucy said. "Claims the club is not her scene."

"I'm with her. So who's the blonde hanging on her hubby and my ex?"

"That's the new owner, Elizabeth 'Call me Liz' Cady," Lucy said.

Lolly squinted. "Looks pretty chummy with the swashbuckler there. What's with the ponytail anyway? Does Pam like that look?"

Lucy laughed. "Claims he's cutting it soon."

Harriet gazed over at the group. "I think he looks gorgeous."

"Of course he does," Lolly said. "That's the trouble. Since it looks like we'll be here a while, anyone for another drink?"

All three stood. "We'll come with you," Lucy said. "Maybe we can take our drinks to the deck?"

As they passed the stage, Lolly caught her sister's eye and gave her a thumbs-up."

Marla nodded as she belted out a soulful tune.

A few minutes later, drinks in hand, Harriet said, "You two head out to the deck. I just want to check with Kyle."

The partners strolled to the end of the dock, the music fading into the background, sounds eclipsed by the crashing of the waves around them. "Any word?" Lucy said.

Lolly shook her head. "Nope. He has a girlfriend. Says it's over, but they still own a place together. Never really over in cases like that."

"You don't know that."

"Well, I know he's not Mr. Reliable."

"Don't give up on him yet, sweetie."

"I barely know him. There's no giving up, 'cause there was nothing there."

"I saw a spark. That's something."

"Okay, Ms. Pollyanna, you dream on and see where it gets you."

Harriet joined them, and the three sat side by side on benches at the end of the dock. "Kyle'll come and find us soon. Richard too," she said.

Lolly sighed, gazing up at a clear starry sky. "What a beautiful night!"

"Sure is," the sisters echoed over the sounds of the sea.

CHAPTER 15

When Jack parked at the hospital, he sighed, resting his head on the Volvo's steering wheel, wondering what he'd find past the emergency room's gleaming glass doors. Once inside, he was led to a curtained enclosure where she lay curled in a fetal position, impossibly thin, heedless to the tubes and apparatus strapped to her arm.

"Poppy?"

She raised her head and lay flat on her back, staring up at the ceiling. Ripped jeans and a filthy T-shirt were draped on the chair beside her. Her hair fell in tangled clumps around birdlike shoulders. There wasn't a trace of the nationally-ranked varsity soccer player she'd been several years earlier other than emaciated but still well-delineated calves peeking out from under her johnny. A knee injury, subsequent addiction to prescription drugs, and uncontrolled bulimia had ended her career.

"What the hell happened here?" he asked, instantly regretting his sharp tone.

"Fuck you," she spat back, turning away.

"What happened?" he asked the nurse.

"A couple of her friends dumped her outside."

"Are they here now?"

"No, they hightailed it. She was vomiting blood, and they were spooked."

Nice friends, he thought. "What's her condition?"

"I'll get the attending physician. Excuse me."

"The nurse disappeared, and Poppy stared at the wall, refusing to meet his gaze. "They told me I could call someone."

"What about your mom?"

"She told me she never wants to see me again."

"She was worried about the baby. She didn't mean it. I talked to her earlier. She's concerned."

"Yeah, right."

"Where have you been staying?"

"Here and there."

"Well, you need to go home."

"Why? You left. You know what she's like."

"You're sick, Poppy. You need to go home and heal."

A tall bespectacled man in green scrubs pulled back the curtain. "Hello, I'm Dr. Downey. Are you Poppy's dad?"

Jack shook his head. "Just a friend."

"Oh? I was under the impression one of her parents was coming."

"I'm here at the request of her mother. How is she?"

"Legally, we're only supposed to confer with family."

Jack took a deep breath. "Give me a break, will you? Listen, I got the call and just drove an hour to get here. Is she able to go home?"

"She's stable. We've pumped her full of fluids and given her meds to calm the stomach. The pregnancy complicates things with bulimia. She's in pretty rough shape for a kid her age."

"I'm right here, you know?" Poppy said, propping up on one elbow.

Downey turned to her. "Sorry, of course. Ms. Blake, you need treatment at a good outpatient facility if you don't want to end up here every week. Your bulimia appears to be out of your control. Your mouth, throat, and stomach are inflamed and damaged. They need time and treatment if they're to heal. And you've got to think of your child too."

Jack turned to the physician. "Can we have a couple of minutes?"

"Sure thing."

When the curtain closed, he said, "Look, Poppy. I can take you to your mom's. Is that what you want?"

"I want to stay with you."

"Well, that's not possible. I'm in the company condo and am not allowed to have overnight guests," he lied. *No telling what she'd rip off the walls while I'm sleeping. What a nightmare.* Truth was he didn't know Marsha's troubled daughter very well. He and her mother had gotten together long after her issues had begun, and Poppy had been in and out of rehab for the two years he'd known her. "Besides, you heard the doc. You're really sick. You need treatment. That's something you and your mom will need to work out. I'll phone her."

"Big whoop."

"Be right back."

He phoned Marsha and after a tortured back-and-forth, she said, "Of course bring her here, duh!" and clicked off.

The drive into the city was mostly silent, any attempt on his part to draw her into conversation futile. Miraculously, he found a spot on the street in front of the condo. He parked and looked over at her. "Listen, Poppy. We don't know each other well, but if there's a way I can help, will you let me know?"

"Yeah, right, as if you care."

"I do care. You're hurting, and I want you to get well for you and the child."

"No one can help me now." The thin, reedy voice was heartbreaking.

"What about your dad?"

"Surely you jest? He's a thousand times more useless than Marsha."

From everything he knew about Chuckie Blake, he was pretty sure she spoke the truth. "Well, look. If you're ready to get treatment, maybe a long-term program, I can help."

"Maybe." Her hand was on the door handle now.

"Okay then, I'll walk you in."

"You don't have to."

"I want to. Come on," he said as the front door to the complex opened and Marsha appeared.

For once, Marsha decided to tone it down. As Poppy climbed the steps, she spoke gently, placing her arms around her daughter's thin shoulders. "Come on, then." As Poppy disappeared inside, Marsha gazed down at him, standing at the bottom of the steps. "You coming in?"

"Not this time."

"Figures."

"I told her I'd help if she decides to get treatment."

"That's big of you."

"Night, Marsha. Good luck."

"Fuck you, Jack," she said, turning away and slamming the door behind her.

That's the second time I've heard that tonight, he thought. *Time to step away. Might be worth giving her the condo to make a clean break.* He resolved to talk to his lawyer on Monday. He would have Jay set up a trust for Poppy's care and arrange to transfer ownership of the condo to Marsha. *Geez, what a mess!*

CHAPTER 16

Jack breathed a contented sigh as he stepped inside the cottage, dropping his duffel by the door. *Home*, he thought, *or at least the place that feels most like home right now.* He wondered how much of that feeling was related to his neighbors to the west. Grabbing a light jacket, he headed for the back door, deciding that a beach walk was what he needed.

At low tide, the craggy shore was exposed, deserted, late-afternoon shadows playing over the rocks, and mounds of seaweed dotting the sand. He breathed in the salty breeze and decided he could get used to this. All the years in the city, he'd missed the water. Maybe it was time to buy a place at the beach. Maybe not Maine, but closer to Boston? An undiscovered treasure only an hour's drive away, the village of Horseshoe Crab Cove might be just the spot. A place for Lyddie and Jack Junior to visit when they weren't with their mother in Maine?

After walking as far as he could before the way was barred by stone outcroppings and the surging tide, he turned and headed back, pausing to sit on a flat boulder, gazing out across the river at the distant shore. *Yup, I could get used to this.*

As he climbed the path to the trail leading back to the cottage, he realized he had very little in the refrigerator. *Guess I'll head into town.*

He'd heard good things about the Grille from Lindsay Barnes. *Lindsay...gotta call Lindsay*, he mused, but decided it could wait until Monday. Head down, lost in thought, he almost collided with mother and daughter as he emerged from the path.

"Hi, Jack!" Maisie said, beautiful brown eyes sparkling.

He grinned, looking from woman to child. "Good to see you ladies."

"We're going for a beach walk before Daddy picks me up! I'm having a sleepover."

"Good for you. Hi," he said, turning to her mother.

"You're back." Her violet eyes were wary, one eyebrow arched. In jeans and T-shirt that hugged her gorgeous body, she looked lovely. Earthy, warm, and sensual, even though she was looking at him like he had the bubonic plague.

"Just. Took a walk to clear my head."

"Good trip?"

He shrugged. "It's over. Glad to be back. Hey, I was thinking of heading into town for supper. Don't suppose you'd like to join me after Maisie's dad comes?"

"Thanks, but we just ate," Lolly said.

"Another time, then. Whaddya think my chances are of getting a table at that Grille place?"

She grinned. "Might be tricky. It's Saturday night. You could probably eat at the bar."

"Fine with me."

"Hold up, Maisie!" she called as the child disappeared around a bend in the path. "Have you got your phone with you?"

Puzzled, he reached into his pocket. She took it and punched in a number. "Hey, Vince, this is Lolly...okay, yeah, I'm fine. Have you got a table for a friend of mine? Or space at the bar? You have? Great...the name's Jack. Yup, see ya." She clicked off and handed him the iPhone. "All set."

He smiled. "Impressive. Wish you could come with me."

She nodded, stepping back. "Enjoy your dinner. Got to catch up with my daughter before she falls off a cliff."

He watched as she hurried down the path, admiring her glorious round ass. *The woman is perfect. A goddess.*

~

THE GRILLE WAS PACKED, BUT THE MINUTE HE GAVE HIS NAME, HE WAS ushered to a small table in the corner. "Unless you'd prefer the bar?" the maître d' asked, turning to face him.

"Actually, I would," Jack said. "Save this for a nice couple who wants privacy."

He settled in and ordered a martini. *Why not, after the last twenty-four hours?*

"Jack, is that you?" a voice said from behind. He turned to find Lucy Morgan on the arm of a tall, slender man with thick salt-and-pepper hair and the bushiest eyebrows he'd ever seen.

Jack stood up, turning to greet them. "Ms. Morgan, hello."

She smiled, her pale-blue eyes dancing with light. "None of that 'Ms. Morgan' business. It's Lucy, and this is my husband, Richard. Richard, this is Jack Faulkner."

Richard came forward and gave him a firm handshake. "Great to meet you, Mr. Faulkner. I may have heard a story or two about the town's newest arrival. And before you reply, it's Richard or Dick."

"It's Jack," he said, grinning as he observed the interplay between the couple.

Lucy gave her husband a nudge. "Don't pay attention to a word he says. Oh, and here's Wolfie, Richard's youngest. He runs our winery."

"Hey," Wolfie said, stepping forward to shake Jack's hand.

"Hello," Jack said, gazing from father to son. Richard's offspring bore little resemblance to his father, with his piercing coal-black eyes, long dark hair, and thick beard. With his strong, broad shoulders, he reminded Jack of the actor Jason Momoa. He half expected to spy Aquaman's scales at the base of the man's neck, his shirt collar open.

"Join us, why don't you?" Lucy said. "It's just us three, and we have plenty of room at our table."

"I don't want to bust in on a family dinner," he said.

Richard clapped him on the shoulder. "Nonsense, we have 'em every night. Come on, we'd love it. Have you ordered?"

"Just sat down."

"Then it's settled," she said, waving to the bartender. "Vincent, we're snatching Jack!"

CHAPTER 17

They all ordered different pasta dishes and had the waiter set them in the middle of the table so they could share. Lucy had ordered pumpkin ravioli with capers and a light cream sauce, which Jack would have gladly consumed in its entirety. He had a special fondness for ravioli, and his lobster ravioli with pink sauce didn't disappoint. He'd actually groaned with pleasure at his first bite. "This is the best pasta I've ever eaten."

Lucy smiled. "All made here. Rosa's recipes. You should see what she does around the holidays. She dyes the dough and makes the most beautiful designs, almost too beautiful to eat."

Richard winked. "But we manage. "So, Jack, Lucy tells us you're in negotiations to buy the Barnum place."

"Something like that. It's a work in progress."

"When we first moved to town, I was tempted to buy the place myself. So many possibilities."

"And a lot of work. Sounds like you have projects of your own between the winery and stables."

"And the newest Morgan's Fire venture," Lucy said. "A farm-to-table restaurant."

"Really?" Jack said, looking from one to the other. "Is it part of the winery?"

Richard grinned. "Let's just say that they complement each other. It's the brainchild of my new son-in-law, Sandy Rodriguez, son of the owners of this very establishment."

"Small town," Jack said, twirling an excellent linguini aioli round his fork.

Richard nodded. "Yup. Sandy sold his very successful music venue up the coast a few months ago and was looking for a new project. He and my daughter Pam came to us with a proposal to buy a large parcel of land for the restaurant and a small farm."

Lucy squeezed her husband's hand. "How could we refuse?"

"I've worked on a couple of projects like that. They're very cool. My favorite places to eat too, although this place is pretty spectacular."

"The Grille might as well be marketed as farm-to-table. Most of the food comes from local farms," Wolfie said.

"I bet my son-in-law would love your input," Richard said.

"Happy to help while I'm around," Jack said. "And, I'd love a tour of the winery. It's always been a secret dream of mine to have vineyards."

"Anytime," Wolfie said. "It's a work in progress too."

They spent the rest of the meal sharing stories about the farm and Jack's plans for Barnum's Ledge. Richard insisted upon picking up the check. While he and Wolfie were at the bar settling up, Lucy and Jack wandered out to the sidewalk, standing under one of the lanterns that lit Main Street after dark. "I tried to get your partner to join me tonight," he said.

"And?"

"And she blew me off, told me she'd already eaten."

Lucy smiled. "Probably true. This is Maisie's weekend with her dad, but Pam and Sandy were meeting with Richard just before we came to dinner so they dropped her off for dinner with Lolly. Sandy told me he was on his way to pick Maisie up."

"I blew it, didn't I?"

"Excuse me?"

"With Lolly. Canceling the music thing."

"I'm sure she understood."

He raised an eyebrow. "I'm not so sure."

"Give it another try. She might surprise you."

He shrugged, grinning. "Thanks for letting me crash your dinner."

"Are you kidding? My husband was in heaven. Wolfie too. They were serious about getting you out to the farm about the restaurant project. I shouldn't say this, but if you don't want to get swallowed up, I'd put some boundaries up there or risk getting carried away by the Morgan tsunami. It's pretty powerful."

Jack laughed. "Your husband is not unknown to me. He's kind of a legend in the business world."

"So I hear."

"Well, I'm happy to help depending on how the Barnum's Ledge project develops."

"There's my new best friend," Richard said, slapping him on the back. "Whenever you're free, come out, and we'll give you the five-cent farm tour."

"And the hundred-dollar winery visit," Wolfie said, grinning.

"In fact, are you free for dinner this week? We'd love to have you join us, wouldn't we, darling?"

"Absolutely," Lucy said.

"I'd really like that. I'm pretty open," Jack said, handing her his card. "Why don't you figure out a good night, and I'll be there."

"I'll be in touch tomorrow," she said. "Have a good night."

"You too," he said, watching as the three strolled down the darkened street before disappearing around the corner.

He hopped into his SUV, which was parked just across the street, and picked up his cell phone. Four missed calls from Marsha, one from Lindsay Barnes, and one from his daughter Lydia. Ignoring the others, he punched in Lyddie's number.

CHAPTER 18

"Hey, Dad," she said, always cheerful.

"Hey, punky, how you doin'?"

"Great. It's been an awesome time up here, but I'm ready to head back to sanity. Mom's driving me a bit crazy, asking about my future."

"That's a parent's job, right?"

"Ha-ha. You don't do that...at least as not much. Listen, I was thinking of crashing with you for a week or so."

"Of course, always, but I'm not home right now. Were you counting on Boston?"

"Not necessarily. Where are you?"

He explained about the Barnum's Ledge project and described the village. "And I'm staying in a beautiful cottage. Has two bedrooms and it's a five-minute walk to a very cool beach."

"I'm in!"

"Great, when are you coming?" As he chatted, he gazed down and spied the flyer for the Merlin's Closet mystery weekend. Lyddie was an avid mystery reader, and they often shared their newest discoveries. Cynthia, her mother, was too.

"Thursday or Friday. Does that work?"

"Perfect. Hey, I've got an idea. A local bookstore is putting on a mystery readers' weekend. Flyer says Friday night and Saturday. You interested? I could sign us up."

"I would love that!"

They chatted a few minutes longer, then hung up. As he started the car to drive back to the cottage, he began humming. A week with Lyddie was just what he needed after the Poppy/Marsha quagmire.

THE NOW-FAMILIAR LUMP IN HER THROAT, LOLLY WAVED GOODBYE AS Maisie drove off with her father and Pam. These were the loneliest moments of her week. As the truck disappeared around the bend in the drive, she turned to head inside. She sighed, deciding that there was still plenty of daylight for a walk. Instead of the beach, she decided to take the path that wound behind Mavis's mansion before connecting to the village's Loop Trail. Once on the Loop, you could walk about a mile, then descend the rise to a trail that ended at the edge of the village. From there, it was an easy mile walk home on the road.

Pitch-dark as she headed back, Lolly climbed the estate's winding driveway, wondering for the hundredth time why her mother hadn't installed at least a few street lights. Aside from the lighting trained on the Cove Inn and Spa sign, the road was dark all the way to Netherfield Manor, not to mention the cottage driveways. The walk had lifted her spirits, and as she proceeded, she thought about the mystery she was halfway through, looking forward to curling up in her cozy living room.

She'd just reached the crest of the hill when headlights shone behind her. Assuming it was her mother back from an evening jaunt, she turned, shielding her eyes from the glare of high beams. *Definitely not Mom's Mercedes. Who could it be?* As he drew up alongside her, she mumbled, "Of course. Him."

"Evening," he called. "Good thing you're wearing that white sweater. I could've hit you."

"Not if I jumped into the bushes first."

He laughed. "Can I give you a lift?"

"No, thanks. I'm almost home."

"How about coming to my place for a nightcap or cup of tea?"

"Nothing personal. Just not a great time. Have a good night." With that, she stalked off, immediately swallowed up by the night.

Jack sat for a minute, shaking his head. *Yup, definitely mad. Shortest romance I've ever had.*

Back at the cottage, he grabbed a beer and his phone and headed out to the screened-in porch. *No sense stalling. Better to get the calls over with now.*

He called Lindsay Barnes first. "Hey, Jack, so glad to hear from you. I've been worried. I wondered about dinner tonight, but couldn't reach you."

"Sorry. I just got back."

"How about tomorrow? Sunday brunch? Ballard's up the coast has a fabulous Sunday brunch."

"Have you got a counteroffer for me?" he asked, weary of the back-and-forth, not to mention the woman's relentless flirting.

"Not yet, but that doesn't stop us from having some fun, getting to know each other?"

"This is business, Lindsay. I make it a rule never to mix business with other things. I never socialize with clients."

"But I'm not your client," she drawled in her best come-hither voice.

"You represent the sellers. The ball's in their court, by the way."

"They promised to get back to me tomorrow."

"Great, well, let me know how that goes."

"So I guess brunch is out?"

"Yup."

"Well then, why don't we set up a meeting for Monday morning? My office, ten o'clock?"

"Sounds good. See you then. Enjoy your weekend." He clicked off, forestalling any further conversation.

Real estate was a game, and he'd danced this waltz dozens of times. Barnum's Ledge was a terrific property, but somehow, his heart wasn't in it like it usually would be. *What the hell's wrong with me? Lolly Rogers, that's what.* He morosely sipped his beer. At the moment, getting her to speak to him was much more important than nailing down Barnum's Ledge. After reviewing the preliminary cost projections, Roland had given him the go-ahead and the top bid he could offer, but all he wanted was to put his arms around a certain violet-eyed beauty and bury his face in her glorious ample cleavage. He gave his head a shake. *Idiot! You have a crew depending upon the months of work the resort would require. Get your head back in the game. Now!*

He cringed as he made his next call.

"It's about time!" she snapped. No *"Hello,"* no *"How are you?"*

"Sorry, Marsha, it's been a really busy day. What's up?"

"What's up is our daughter's a mess, and I need help."

He sighed, refraining from correcting the "our daughter" part. "What about her dad? Have you phoned Chuck?"

"Surely you jest."

"Look, Marsha, I'm happy to help with the rehab costs."

"That's big of you. The sooner you wash your hands of this, the better?"

You've got that right, he thought, willing his voice to be calm. "And, Marsha, I've spoken to Jay," he said, referring to his attorney. "He's drawing up papers to deed the condo over to you."

"And how the hell am I supposed to afford to keep it up?"

Get a job. She was an attorney, but had quit her job at a prestigious law firm two months after they started living together. "That's a decision you'll have to make—sell or stay—but at least it will be an asset for you."

"I know what you're doing, trying to buy me off."

"Marsha, it's over. We both agreed it was over months ago."

"Well, I never did! Whatever. Poppy's checking into Farrell Park tomorrow. It's a clinic and rehab place in Northboro. Very nice, highly recommended."

"Great. I hope this helps her get back to normal."

"Us together would really help."

Not gonna happen. "Let me know what I can contribute. I hope Chuck's helping there."

"He will once I call him. Jack, I really want to see you."

"Sorry, I'm out of town for at least a month or two. Buried in work."

"And where is that?"

"I've gotta go, Marsha. Take care. I'll have Jay contact you about the condo transfer. Night." He clicked off, wondering if he should get a new cell number or figure out how to block calls.

Before heading in, he texted Pete Santoro asking him to meet at two the following day. He knew it was an imposition for his foreman, but Pete and his roommate, Al, were staying the weekend in Bayport —some plan about Al and surfing—so he hoped a brief meeting wouldn't screw up their day too much. If the project went forward, he'd have to make arrangements for the crew to stay in the area, at least during the week, unless they preferred to go home. Most didn't. After making a list, he headed inside, grabbed one of the mysteries Lolly had given him, and hoped it would put him to sleep.

CHAPTER 19

Sunday morning, Jack ate breakfast at the Café, then wandered down Main Street and into Laura's Community Garden. There were several gardeners tending to their raised beds and a short woman in a large straw hat, rubber boots, and overalls watering. As he approached, she waved. "Good morning."

"What an incredible spot," he said. "Are you in charge?"

She laughed, a deep throaty laugh as she switched off the hose. "Strictly volunteer."

As she turned to face him, Jack was surprised to find she was a young woman, not much older than his kids, petite and thin, with wispy blonde hair poking out from under her hat. Her mischievous blue eyes danced with light. "Jack Faulkner," he said, extending his hand. "New in town."

"Kitty Bannister, landscaper and loyal volunteer."

"I've heard your name," he said. "You designed this space, didn't you?"

She smiled. "Guilty as charged, but truthfully, it was a group effort and, of course, Pam Morgan Rodriguez's inspiration."

"Named after her mother," he said, remembering Lindsay's description. When he'd asked about local landscapers, Kitty's had been one of the names the Realtor had given him.

"For a new guy, you're pretty well informed."

He grinned. "I get around, and I'm nosey. I may be restoring a property in the village and will really need a landscape designer. You wouldn't happen to have a business card on you, would you?"

"No, but my studio's over there," she said, pointing toward the hardware store parking lot. "If you hang on a few minutes, I'll walk back and get one."

"You got it. Anything I can do while I'm waiting?"

"There's a wheelbarrow of clippings that needs to get dumped in the compost pile." She pointed again, this time toward the north edge of the garden.

"Consider it done."

After dumping his load, he sat on a bench in the shade, watching the beehive of activity as more gardeners arrived to tend their plots. As he watched, his mind turned to Barnum's Ledge and their landscaping needs. Lost in thought, he was startled by Kitty Bannister's voice behind him. "Ready, Mr. Faulkner?"

"Jack, please," he said, rising and following her out the garden's west gate.

"This gate was a last-minute addition," she said, "but it's made all the difference. Easy for me. Besides, most of the gardeners park in the hardware store lot. My uncle doesn't mind. That's the one thing we didn't consider in the planning. Parking."

They stepped into her wide-open studio, tables covered with blueprints and drafting supplies. It seemed a bit disorganized to Jack, but he was kind of a neat freak. Marsha, one of the messiest people in the world, had driven him crazy with piles and clutter everywhere.

"Here you go," she said, handing him her card. "I can see by your expression that you're not a fan of my housekeeping."

He chuckled. "Am I that transparent?"

"No worries, I'm very organized on my landscaping designs and projects."

"I'm not worried, and I'll be in touch if the project moves forward."

"Barnum's Ledge has incredible possibilities." When she saw his look of astonishment, she added, "Small town. Everyone knows your business. Better get used to it."

"Well, thanks, Kitty. I've got a meeting, so I have to run."

Removing her hat and wiping dirt from her brow, she gave him a crooked smile. "No prob. See you soon, I hope."

PETE WAS SITTING ON THE PORCH WHEN HE ARRIVED. "SORRY!" HE called, climbing the porch steps.

"Just got here," his foreman said, "and it's never a chore enjoying this view."

"Pretty spectacular, isn't it?" He sat down at the small table, facing the other man. "Wait till you hear my new ideas for it."

The men spent several hours talking, and when they parted company, Jack decided to stay and walk down to the beach below the ledge. The bay was glassy and calm, a slight breeze blowing from the east as he made his way down the rickety steps that ran along the cliff face. When he reached the sand, he threw off his shoes, loving the feel of warm sand between his toes. The beach was deserted, walled off to the east and west by rock outcroppings that would only allow safe passage at low tide. Jack found a sunny spot, lay down, and, before long, fell asleep. An hour later, he woke to waves lapping his feet.

When he got back to the cottage, he called his boss and outlined his new ideas for the property. Not surprisingly, Roland Jenkins gave him the green light. "A long as you're sure. I trust you to know what you're doing. Let me know how the final negotiations go tomorrow."

"Will do," Jack said, hanging up. "Now for dinner," he said aloud. He decided to risk rejection again and phoned Lolly, but her phone went straight to voicemail. He had enjoyed the meal he and Lolly had shared at the Bluewater so he jumped back into the SUV and headed out.

The Bluewater was hopping, the parking lot overflowing onto the streets in both directions. The bar again, he mused, parking a short distance down the road and walking.

After waiting a few minutes, he found a seat at the bar and ordered a beer and a menu. He'd just ordered fish and chips when Lindsay Barnes slid onto the stool beside him. "Small world," she said, giving him her best come hither smile.

And getting smaller all the time. "Lindsay, hey."

"What brings you out here?"

"Gotta eat."

"Are you with someone?"

"Nope, how about you?"

She waved her empty wineglass at the waiter, then turned to him. "There's a group of us that meet every Sunday night. Sometimes other nights as well. They're out on the porch. Would you like to join us?" She nudged against him, already slightly tipsy.

"Thanks, but I've already ordered. I've got lot of work, so I'm just having a quick bite."

"Surely you have time for one little drink?" she purred. As she leaned closer, he feared her ample breasts might fall out of her T-shirt's low scoop neck.

"Thanks, but I'll pass."

"Then I'll stay right here and keep you company," she said, now plastered to his side.

Something will have to be done about this, he thought, standing. "Let me speak to the bartender, then I'll walk you back to your friends."

"Party pooper," she slurred as he asked the bartender to save his spot.

Once he deposited Lindsay at her table, telling her that he'd see her in the morning, he hurried back in and asked for his dinner to go. No telling what she'd be like the next time she passed by. As he carried his to-go box out, he spied her heading in, scanning the room for him, and managed to duck out just in time.

CHAPTER 20

Monday morning as Jack headed into town for his meeting with Lindsay Barnes, his cell phone rang.

"Hey, Jack, it's Lucy Morgan."

"Good morning," he said, then braked hard as a deer leapt out in front of him and disappeared into the woods at the edge of the road. "Geez!"

"Are you okay?"

"Yes, near miss with a very large doe."

"This area's teeming with them. Gotta be careful. Can you talk, or shall I call you back?"

"I'm fine. Shoot."

"Richard and I wanted to invite you to dinner tomorrow night. Are you free?"

"Yes, and I'd love to come. What can I bring?"

"Just yourself. Around six? It's a family dinner, so we try to eat earlier for the kids."

"Sounds perfect. Hey, Lucy, before you go. I'd like to sign up for your mystery weekend, if there are still openings?"

"There are, and we'd love it. There's a reception Friday night and workshops all day Saturday, with the closing dinner Saturday night. Shall I sign you up for everything?"

"Sounds great. Please make the reservation for two people, and I'll get the payment to you tomorrow night."

"Will do. And no hurry on the payment. You can even settle up Friday. The opening reception is here at the farm."

"Terrific, I'm...we're looking forward to it."

"In the spirit of the mystery, we use pseudonyms. How would you like to be listed?"

Jack chuckled, saying the first thing that came to mind. "How about George and Martha McDoogle?"

Lucy laughed. "George and Martha it is! See you tomorrow."

He rang off and, a few minutes later, pulled into the small Village Realty lot. *Here goes nothing*, he thought, bracing himself.

"THIS IS ENOUGH FOR TODAY," LUCY ANNOUNCED, HANDS ON HIPS AS she gazed at her partner. Buried in their preparations for Merlin's Closet Mystery Weekend, they were working in the main barn at Morgan's Fire, now jokingly referred to as the "town function venue" as Richard and his family generously opened the doors for many local gatherings. "What about a glass of wine on the porch?"

"Love it. I'll bring the attendees list, and we can go over while we sip."

Lucy smiled as she led the way into the house. After listening to several days of Lolly's complaining about men, particularly about Jack Faulkner and his unreliability, they'd been so busy, the subject of the list hadn't come up. Lucy was in charge of keeping the roster of attendees and had printed out copies, but they hadn't yet discussed them together. As they walked, she said, "I hope you're still planning to join us for dinner tomorrow night?"

"Are you sure? It's your family dinner and all."

"Positive."

"Maisie's so excited. She loves Sasha, Cam, and Laura," Lolly said, referring to Richard's daughter Ava's three children ages eight, seven, and five respectively.

"And they love her. It'll be fun."

They stepped into the kitchen, where they found Richard chatting with their housekeeper and cook, Callie Richardson. Callie had been with the family for most of her life. Blonde and slender, with blue eyes, she was a widow. Her husband had succumbed to cancer not long after Richard's first wife, Laura.

"Hi, ladies," Richard said, rising from his stool and coming to hug his wife. "How are you doing out there?"

"Lots of progress," Lolly said. "It's gonna be great."

Lucy returned his embrace, then headed for one of the room's three refrigerators. "We're heading out to the porch with wine and cheese."

"I'll bring out a cheese tray," Callie said, hopping up.

"Bless you," Lucy said, grabbing a bottle of sauvignon blanc. "By this time next year, we'll be enjoying a bottle of Morgan's Fire White. You two want to join us?"

"Thanks, but I'm in the middle of dinner prep," Callie said.

"And I'm off to the stables," he said. "If you're still out there when I get back, I'm in."

The two women settled in porch rockers, the fiery-orange evening sky in front of them. Lolly sighed. "I love this time of night. My mother drives me crazy, but it's times like this that I'm incredibly grateful she's close by."

"Sleepover?"

"Yup, and I suspect there'll be more as the week progresses. So let's see this list. Wow, we're up to sixty-five people! Almost to our cutoff."

Lucy nodded. "I hope this is it, at least for those from far away." They had capped the weekend at seventy-five. Fortunately, most of the attendees were local as the village didn't have a great many choices for accommodations. The few out-of-towners were booked at local B and Bs and a few at a motel in Bayport.

Lolly frowned as she read down the list. "George and Martha McDoogle? Who the hell are they?"

Her partner grinned, taking a sip of her wine. "Latecomers."

"Do we know them?"

"Him yes, her no."

Lolly stared at her. "I see that mischievous look. Who are they?"

"Wouldn't you rather be surprised?"

"No!"

"Well...okay, then. It's Jack and a friend."

"Jack Faulkner?"

"Yup."

"Well, that's just great! Just what I need to make the weekend a complete disaster. First my ex and his perfect wife are keeping Maisie all weekend. She'll probably never want to come home. And now this? Who is he bringing?"

"He didn't say and I didn't ask."

"Well, why the hell not?"

"He didn't offer, and I didn't want to pry."

"Fine. I can handle this. I got through the wedding. I can certainly get through our resident Lothario parading around with his bimbo."

"How do you know she's a bimbo? Besides, you told me yesterday that you'd washed your hands of him."

"I have! I can be civil, professional, cordial, and everything in between. Just watch me."

Grinning like the Cheshire Cat, Lucy held out the tray of olives, cheeses, and crackers that Callie had brought them. "Good, because I invited him to dinner tomorrow night."

"What!"

"It was Richard's idea. He wants Jack's input on the farm-to-table project. And Sam's joining us. You know Jack wants to meet him. If Barnum's Ledge goes through, he wants to hire him."

"Well, I'll have to beg out."

"Oh no, you won't. You just said that Maisie is really excited, and Ava and Dan's kids are too. You're coming, and that's that."

Lolly fumed as she drove home, knowing she was stuck going to the dinner the following evening. Maisie loved the farm and Richard's grandchildren. She couldn't back out now. Truth be told, even while leery of getting further involved with Jack, she'd been disappointed not to bump into him around the cottages, beach, or in town. *What's the matter with me?* she thought morosely as she turned in to her mother's estate. She considered driving up to Netherfield and grabbing Maisie so she wouldn't be alone, but the thought of a long leisurely bath and a good book won out.

As she passed the driveway that led to Jack's cottage, she spied lights and felt a twinge of sadness remembering his kisses, his beautiful kind eyes, and the rest of his solid, gorgeous body. *Another dream*, she mused, parking the battered old Volvo and heading inside.

CHAPTER 21

Jack leaned back on the porch glider, closing his eyes, wondering whether his new plan for Barnum's Ledge was crazy or perhaps the sanest idea he'd come up with yet. At this stage of his career with Compass, Roland considered him more like a partner, and his salary reflected his boss's trust and high esteem. He'd done very well with what Roland liked to call his "boutique development company." Over the years, they'd taken many historic properties and turned them into elegant resort destinations for the wealthy elite who valued small and private.

As he glided back and forth, the sounds of the night surrounded him—owls screeching, coyotes howling, and trees rustling. *It's peaceful here. I could get used to this.* He wondered if there might be a place at Barnum's Ledge for him. In truth, he could work from anywhere, and once he divested himself of Marsha and the condo, there was little keeping him in Boston. As if on cue, his cell rang, and Marsha's high-pitched screech shook him from his reverie.

As Marsha rambled on, he spied a lone figure crossing the back field. Her flashlight beam played along the ground as she headed toward her home. *A little late for a beach walk,* he mused as Marsha's voice called him back.

"Jack? Are you listening to me?"

"Sorry, got distracted. You were saying?"

"I was saying what are you going to do about this situation?"

He took a deep breath. "What situation is that?" he asked, knowing full well he was about to hear more of the same. For the life of him, he couldn't recall what had attracted him to the whining harridan on the other end of the line. Had she always been this shrill?

"Poppy, of course. She keeps asking for you."

"I thought Farrell Park discouraged outside contact."

"Every case is different."

Jack counted to ten. Things were descending into craziness now, with no end in sight. Clearly, Marsha was no longer rational and needed professional help. *Maybe I need professional help? Time to get Jay involved, block her calls, prohibit all contact.* "Marsha, I barely know Poppy. I can't believe her caregivers at Farrell Park would encourage her mother's ex-boyfriend, who is nothing more than an acquaintance, to get involved."

"Fuck them. Poppy is asking for you, and that's all that matters. Or don't you care if she ever gets better?"

"Give me a break, Marsha. You and I both know I'm not the key to Poppy's recovery."

"Of course you aren't, you never will be, but she's my daughter, she's hurting, and she's asking for *you*. Not me and not her father."

"Look, I'll phone Farrell Park in the morning and see what they have to say, okay?"

"No, but it will have to do."

"Well, you take care."

"I heard from your vulture Jay Hallowell today."

More deep breaths as he braced himself. "Oh?"

"What a lowlife."

Jack wasn't getting into a conversation about his close friend, who had been his attorney since their college days. "Great, he said he's arranging the transfer of ownership and will get it to me to sign this week."

"So you're meeting with him, then?"

"He's my friend. We meet almost every week, as you well know."

"So he can know where you are, but your longtime partner can't?"

"Listen Marsha, I've got to run. I'll be in touch soon about the condo, and I'll call Farrell Park tomorrow. Take care."

He clicked off, then phoned Jay. When his friend answered, he said, "Hey, buddy, I may need your advice on restraining orders."

After they discussed a number of options for what they now referred to as "the Marsha problem," they turned to Barnum's Ledge. Jay was handling the closing, and Jack filled him in on his meeting with Lindsay Barnes. He chuckled as his bachelor friend asked about Lindsay.

"Is she hot?"

"Oh, she's hot all right, and she'll be steaming hot for you."

"Then I'll definitely attend the closing in person next week, maybe bring my paddleboards. You game?"

"It'll depend on the day and what's going on. I've got another project here in town."

"Boy, you move fast. What's up?"

"Just consulting. Local people—very rich local people—want to open a restaurant, a very cool one. Farm-to-table."

"This Horseshoe Crab Cove is sounding more and more interesting. Maybe I should come for a night or two. You got room?"

"Ordinarily yes, but Lyddie's in town all next week. But hey, if you're serious, the property where I'm staying has guest rooms in the main building. Gorgeous estate. Right on the water."

"Sounds cool. I'll see if I can shift a few things and come on down. Could use a few days off. Take care and don't worry about the Whip Woman. I'll deal with her."

Jack chuckled. "Yeah, right. Night, buddy."

JACK FAULKNER WAS THE FIRST MAN LOLLY HAD BEEN INTERESTED IN for many years. As she passed through his yard, she saw his shadow on the porch glider and heard his cell phone ring. *Probably his*

girlfriend. After arriving home to an empty house, she decided to walk the path that circled her mother's estate. There was always the danger of encountering coyotes or skunks, but she secretly hoped she might run into her handsome neighbor, the man she'd been stonewalling and avoiding the past few days. Disappointed, she plunged into the woods leading home and left the shadowy figure on the porch to his phone call. She'd see him soon enough, she mused, knowing that she couldn't back out of tomorrow's dinner without crushing her sweet child. *Suck it up, Rogers,* she thought as she made her way to her back door. *A glass of wine, a hot bath, and a good book will set me right! I'll worry about hunky Jack Faulkner and his beautiful blue eyes tomorrow.*

CHAPTER 22

"I have to say, I'm really envious of this incredible property," Jack said as he and Richard Morgan strolled out of the tasting barn after his tour of the winery.

"I've been lucky."

Jack smiled at the man twelve years his senior, who moved with the grace and agility of a twenty-year-old. "I'd guess it's more than luck. You're kind of legend in the business world."

Richard laughed. "Don't believe all you hear. Besides, my son Rich runs everything now. He's the legend these days, and I'm just a cheerleader."

Yeah, right, Jack thought, watching him. The man was a wiry bundle of positive energy.

As they headed for the road leading back to the farmhouse, he pointed east. "Restaurant's gonna be on the bluff. Want to walk up and see the site?"

"Sure."

They headed up a winding path to the top of the rise, gazing down at the river below them. "This is it," Richard said, opening his arms wide. "This is what diners will experience looking out a wall of glass. Sam will know best how to make it happen on paper. Can't wait to see him tomorrow."

Jack whistled. "It's spectacular."

Richard nodded. "We just got the final permits to start grading the site, road, and parking area. I'm thinking clamshells, but it's my son-in-law's decision. His money, his dream."

"Where's the access? They won't all be driving past the house, will they?"

"No way, Jose," his host said, gazing back toward the winery barns. "We didn't walk that way, but behind the storage barn, there's a road that leads to Bayport Pike. Right now it's dirt, but we've decided, with great reluctance, to pave it. Kind of have to with all the trucks and now restaurant traffic. Can't stand paved roads, but it has to be done."

"I hear you, man. There are some cool alternatives to regular asphalt."

Richard nodded. "And don't you know Sandy's already on 'em. Waste of money, in my opinion—pavement is pavement—but don't tell him I said that."

Jack grinned. "Your secret is safe with me."

"Can't wait for you to meet the family. Shall we?" Richard said, gesturing to a path that led south along the top of the bluff.

"What a beautiful night," Lucy said as she stood with her sister, Harriet, and Lolly, watching the children play. Kyle, Harriet's husband and the town veterinarian, chased after the four kids, Weezie Morgan, Richard's youngest daughter on his heels. Kyle's older brother Sam stood on the sidelines, cheering.

"Sure is," Lolly said. "Thanks for having us. Maisie's been dancing up and down all afternoon."

"We love it."

"Where's Richard?" Harriet asked, gazing around at the party that included Weezie's sister Pam and her husband, Sandy, and another Morgan daughter, Ava, and her husband, Dan Fielding. Dan and Ava ran the Horseshoe Crab Cove research facility. Their main focus was the study of the village's namesake, the horseshoe crab, but their charter also included the study of all local marine life and the ecosystems that supported them.

"He's giving our newest town resident a tour of the winery," Lucy said.

Lolly stiffened. "Visitor, you mean?"

Harriet gazed from her sister to her business partner, a puzzled look on her face. "Who?"

Lucy glanced over, spying her partner's frown before saying, "Jack Faulkner."

"Oh, hunky Jack," Harriet said. "I hope they get the property. I love that place. So romantic."

Lucy raised her glass. "Well then, you'll be happy to know that they've come to an agreement. Closing's next week."

"Wow!" her sister said.

"That quickly?" Lolly asked, abandoning any pretense of disinterest.

Lucy nodded. "Apparently, money talks, or Jack's very persuasive. Even Richard was impressed, and you know what a wheeler dealer he is. He's hoping to keep him around as consultant on the restaurant project. Can't wait for him to meet Sandy and Pam."

Lolly gulped. It was all too much. Now this man with whom she was already half in love would no longer be making a hasty retreat, but instead staying on, parading his girlfriends from one end of town to the other, while she stood by and watched, heart in pieces. "Excuse me for a sec, would you?" She set down her wine and turned toward the house.

"You okay, sweetie?" Lucy called.

"Fine, just making a pit stop. Keep an eye on Maisie for me?"

"Will do," Lucy said, shaking her head.

"What's up with her?" Harriet asked.

"She's already crazy about him."

"Really?"

"They moved fast."

"I guess so!"

LOLLY WALKED THROUGH THE FARMHOUSE'S BACKDOOR AND THEN OUT the east door that led down to the barns and stables. She wanted to crawl out of her skin, turn invisible, and disappear. Thoughts of Jack Faulkner moving to the village along with her happily remarried ex-husband were almost too much to bear. Lost in thought, she rounded the stables and ran smack into him.

"Oh!" she cried. "Perfect."

He caught her, wrapping her in an embrace that prevented them both from tumbling to the ground. "Hey," he said softly.

Sputtering, she grounded herself, savoring ten blissful seconds in his arms before pushing back. Her knees wobbled, and she realized she'd been holding her breath, which she let out with a whoosh. "Sorry...so sorry...was...I don't know."

He smiled, the gorgeous smile that only increased his magnetism. It felt to Lolly as if he still held her pressed against him, and she feared she might actually swoon. *This is really too much!* She struggled to collect herself.

"You were somewhere else," he said finally. "Happens to the best of us."

She brushed imaginary straw from her sweater, refusing to meet his gaze. "I thought you were on a tour."

"Just finished. Richard's in the barn talking with his trainer. Listen, Lolly, I'm glad we bumped into each other. I wanted to explain about last weekend."

She raised her arms, pressing her palms facing him. "As I said, there's no need to explain."

"Well, I think there is. There was a woman, Marsha. We're not together and haven't been for many months, but her daughter fell ill, and the hospital called me. I had to pick up Poppy, that's the daughter, and drop her at Marsha's. That and a meeting with my boss kept me in the city, even though I'd much rather have been with you."

"It's fine, Jack. You really don't owe me an explanation, but thank you."

"Don't 'spose you'd consent to dinner tomorrow?"

"Can't. I'm busy."

"Lunch?"

"Sorry, we're swamped getting ready for Mystery Weekend, which I understand you're attending."

"Yes, we—" he started, just as their host stepped out of the barn.

"Hello, my dear," Richard said, giving her a hug and kiss. "You okay? You look a bit flushed."

"I'm fine, just taking a walk."

"Would you like company?" Jack asked.

She linked arms with their host and turned toward the farmhouse. "No, thanks. Walk's over. I'll go back with you guys."

As they headed up the path, the four children flew past them, followed by Marta, Ava and Dan's nanny.

Lolly called, "Marta—do you need help?"

The dark-haired twenty-something laughed, waving. "No, we're fine. Just coming to say hello to the horses. Then we're under strict instructions to come back to have supper."

Jack followed, a bemused expression on his face as they joined the others. Lucy was standing with her sister Harriet. Such a lovely woman, with intense green eyes. As he came alongside Richard and Lolly, his host noticed his gaze. "Have you met Harriet, Lucy's sister? She's a brilliant teacher at Hampton Meeting, a Quaker school north of here. She's married to our village vet, Kyle Morgan."

"Yes, I bumped into them at the Café last week. I've been hearing about Kyle too. I understand you have your own vet on the premises?"

His host nodded. "Kiki Bloom. She's away this week." Richard leaned closer and whispered, "Real spitfire and drop-dead gorgeous. Has all the village ladies in a twitter. My youngest too," he said, pointing to a petite young woman, hair cut short in a dark brown pixie, who had just emerged from under a picnic table with Ava and Dan's youngest, Laura. "Weezie still thinks she's six. She runs the pony camps for us. Ah, and there's my Pammy," he said, pointing to a strawberry blonde, who stood beside a tall, muscular man with long black hair who looked like a walking advertisement for GQ.

Gotta be Sandy Rodriquez, Jack thought as Richard continued. "Those are the two I want to hook you up with. That's my son-in-law, Sandy, with his arm around Pam. And our brilliant architect, Sam. Lolly, can I steal Jack away?"

"Steal away," she said as she headed for Lucy and Harriet.

"That Jack is a cutie, isn't he?" Harriet said.

Lolly gazed at her partner's sister, who was usually reserved and seldom flippant or teasing. "Don't you start."

Lucy smiled as she approached. "So you met up after all."

"Not another word, you two!" Lolly said, taking a big gulp of wine.

THE REST OF THE EVENING WAS FULL OF LIVELY CONVERSATION, THE giggles and shouts of children reverberating from the kitchen where they were eating with Marta and Callie. Jack sat with Pam and Sandy, trading stories and making plans to meet about the restaurant. Wolfie and Weezie were nearby listening and offering suggestions. Lolly sat at the other end of the table with Lucy, Harriet, Kyle, and Richard. Ava and Dan Fielding were positioned in the middle of the table, so they continually switched back and forth between conversations.

Later, as Lolly gathered Maisie, preparing to depart, Jack caught up with them. Lolly could feel his heat, even before she turned to face him.

"Hi, Jack," the child said. "Too bad we didn't drive together. Then we could drop you off."

He smiled, stopping to ruffle her dark curls. "Poor planning. We'll have to remember next time."

"Are we coming again, Mommy? When? When?"

"Come on, Pumpkin," she said, turning to him. "Night."

"Night. You sure about lunch or dinner tomorrow?"

"Very sure. See you Friday night at the welcome dinner. It's casual, by the way, all of it, since we're holding everything except the final dinner here."

"Looking forward to it!"

CHAPTER 23

Wednesday morning, Jack called Farrell Park from the porch of Barnum's Ledge. He was put on hold. As he paced back and forth, he spied Pete's truck in the drive. His foreman was always early, a quality Jack very much appreciated. He waved, pointing to the phone, and Pete disappeared around the back of the building, toolbox in hand.

Finally, a voice came on: "Dr. Stu Collier here. Can I help you?"

He explained the reason for his call, and Collier said, "Uh huh... Yes, I phoned the mother yesterday about this. Seems your stepdaughter is asking for you and is very insistent."

"I'm not her stepfather," Jack said. "Just a family friend."

"Oh, I'm sorry, Mr. Faulkner. She called you that, so I just assumed."

"Honestly, it's a bit of a mess. I'm surprised Farrell Park would allow her contact with anyone, much less someone outside her immediate family."

"This is a clinic. A bit different from a rehab facility. We assess patients on an individual basis rather than insist on hard-and-fast rules. Her therapist, Liza Romano, felt a visit from you might help Poppy."

"A visit?" Jack said. "I thought she wanted me to phone?"

"Liza feels the visit is preferable."

"Listen, Dr. Collier, this is a complicated situation. Quite frankly, I barely know Poppy, and her mother and I are not together and haven't been for a while."

"We're aware of that. Liza suspects that Poppy may be holding this over her mother. I think Liza feels a visit from you and some closure might be beneficial. She's not in now, but will be here by noon. Shall I have her call you?"

"What about this afternoon?"

"Excuse me?"

"What if I came up this afternoon? I'm tied up after that for the next several weeks."

"Well, I guess... I mean, I'm sure we could accommodate you."

They talked awhile longer, and Jack rang off, stating that he would be there by three.

Geez, Louise, he muttered, tossing his phone on the table and heading around the building to find Pete.

"THIS SOUNDS PERFECT, LADIES," LUCY SAID, AS SHE AND LOLLY SAT IN the farmhouse kitchen chatting with Kendall Reese, Mavis LaSalle's chef and Callie.

Lolly looked at her partner. "You sure sixty isn't too many?" I mean...not for these two pros, but that's a lot of people to be running all over your yard and home."

"Ah, have you forgotten the weddings and other events we've hosted here? It's kind of become party central. Richard has the logistics down to a science."

"Yes, but those events were mostly family and close friends," Lolly said, gazing over at Callie. "Gosh, this is great coffee, Call."

The blonde housekeeper winked. "New blend."

Lucy waved several sheets of paper. "Have you looked at the participant list? Most *are* family and friends, or at least we know them."

"If you're okay, I'm okay," Lolly said, not quite successful in keeping the glumness out of her reply.

"You okay, Loll?" Kendall stared at her. The petite strawberry-blonde had piercing green eyes that didn't miss much.

"Fine, just tired," Lolly lied, catching Lucy's eye with a warning glance.

"I think we're set," Lucy said. "Loll and I have to get out to the barn. Any other questions for us?"

Callie shook her head. "We're good. You're going to finalize things with Rosa and Cesar, right?" The Rodriquezes' restaurant was hosting Saturday's dinner in the Grille's large function room on the second floor.

"I'm on it. I'll stop in on my way home. Maisie and I are having lunch on the beach in case anyone wants to join us."

"Sounds heavenly, but Richard wants to have a lunch date at Bluewater, then walk the seawall," Lucy said as they prepared to head out to the barn.

"Thanks. I've got a million things to do around here," Callie said. She was both cook and housekeeper to the large house.

Kendall nodded. "Ditto at my end. Your mom's got a number of guests coming over the weekend and next week, including some friend of Mr. Hunky's."

"Of course, the girlfriend," Lolly muttered, turning away.

"Nope, it's a guy. Coming in Tuesday for a couple of days. He asked about the surfing when he made the reservation."

Lolly chuckled. "Good luck with that! Come on, partner. We've gotta get cracking."

After a couple of hours, arranging tables and chairs and shelving books, Lucy stood back and said, "Merlin's Closet Mystery Weekend is ready to go!" They made a practice of prepping well ahead of events so they could have a day or two before to relax and recharge before the big day. This was no different.

"I think you're right. I'm gonna head off, then. I'll stop at the Grille and make sure everything's all set."

Lucy walked her to the car. "It's going to be fun," she said.

Lolly threw her bag into the front seat. "Yeah, right, with Mr. Hunky flaunting Martha in my face."

"We don't have any idea who Martha is. She might be just a friend."

"And I'm the Easter Bunny. You are ever the optimist, partner of mine," Lolly said, hugging her.

"Always. Have a fun girls' lunch with your little sweetheart."

"Mother has spoiled her so rotten this week she probably won't even want to come."

"Baloney!" Lucy said, patting her shoulder.

AFTER CHATTING WITH CESAR RODRIQUEZ, LOLLY EMERGED FROM THE cool darkness of the Grille, squinting as she stepped into the sunlight on Main Street. As she walked to her car, parked in the Village Hardware lot, she looked ahead and spied Jack and a dark-haired younger man, medium height, muscular build. Too late to change direction, she thought, smiling as they drew near.

"Lolly, hi," he called.

"Hello."

"I don't think you've met my foreman, Pete Santoro?"

"No, hello," she said, extending her hand. His dark eyes danced with light as he took her hand.

"Pleased to meet you," he said, his voice gruff and deep. Not what you'd call handsome, Santoro was rugged, his face tanned and chiseled from hours of outside work. A scar ran along his right jawline to the edge of his smile.

Jack gazed from one to the other, then said, "We're grabbing lunch at the Café if you'd like to join us?"

"Thanks, but Maisie and I are having a beach picnic. Nice to meet you, Pete," she said, hurrying off before her treacherous knees gave way. *Jack Faulkner is danger with a capital D. How will I ever get through the stupid mystery weekend watching him and his bimbo?*

CHAPTER 24

After a quick lunch with Pete, Jack drove back to the cottage and threw things in a duffel. He'd decided to stay the night in the company condo and pack up a few more things for his stay in Horseshoe Crab Cove. Mavis had assured him that Osprey Cottage was his as long as he needed it. She did have wedding bookings, but they could stay at Netherfield or in town. "No need for them to push you out, honey," she assured him.

As he headed out of town, he wondered what he'd find at Farrell Park. He also wondered how he could woo Lolly Rogers. Every time he set eyes on the woman, his libido went into overdrive. Her luscious lips, that long thick hair, her perfect breasts, and those eyes that he could get lost in forever. Hands down, she was the most beautiful and intriguing woman he'd ever met, and she would barely speak to him. *What the hell happened to make her this gun-shy? Sandy Rodriquez seemed like a great guy, and he's certainly devoted to his lovely wife.*

True to its name, Farrell Park was in the middle of a beautiful park on a property of several hundred acres. The main building, a massive stone mansion with turrets, towers, and at least ten chimneys, had once been the home of a wealthy shipbuilding family. Apparently, several members of the family had suffered from bulimia and anorexia, so that when the Farrell family downsized a decade earlier, they had donated the funds and the property to establish the clinic. Farrell Park was now home to one of the country's finest facilities specializing in eating disorders. About a dozen small cottages dotted the landscape around the main building, mostly patients' living quarters.

Jack parked and headed in the main entrance through twelve-foot carved oak doors, their brass fixtures gleaming in the afternoon sun. The receptionist invited him to have a seat while she paged Dr. Collier. The man himself appeared five minutes later.

The tall, lean physician with salt-and-pepper hair extended his hand. "Pleased to meet you, Mr. Faulkner."

"It's Jack," he said, returning Collier's firm handshake.

"Of course. Well, Jack, let me walk you down to Liza's office. I just checked the schedule, and your Poppy is at a yoga class right now."

Jack took a deep breath, trying to stay calm. "As I told you on the phone, I'm happy to help, but she's not my Poppy."

"Of course, shall we?"

Collier led him through the building. Large potted plants stood everywhere, the walls adorned with artwork, and the house's beautiful mahogany woodwork gleaming. They passed a number of offices, what looked like exercise and music rooms, and several open studios, one where the yoga class appeared to be in session. The students all faced the instructor in tree poses. Jack spied Poppy. Under her thin yoga shirt, her back was skeletal.

"Here we are," Collier said as they came to the last office before what appeared to be a dining hall. A slight, dark-skinned woman, her hair falling across her face, was hunched over a laptop screen. She looked up at the sound of her boss's voice. "Liza, here's Jack Faulkner, the friend of the family Poppy's been asking about."

She rose, pushing the laptop aside as she brushed her hair back behind her ears. She was dressed in a red pencil skirt and a crisp white blouse, the top few buttons open revealing a hint of cleavage. "Oh, yes, welcome. Come in."

As Jack stepped into the office, Collier said, "I'll leave you two to carry on, if that's okay?"

"Thanks, Stu," she said, gazing up, giving him an intimate look that wasn't lost on Jack.

Something's going on there, he mused. *Wonder if ole Stu is married?* He took the only other chair in the tiny office. "So how can I help, Ms. Romano?"

"I know this was a big ask, but she keeps going on and on about you, so I thought it might be worth getting you together if for no other reason than to bring closure. I'm getting the impression that Poppy lives in a largely imaginary world because reality may be too painful right now. We've also got the baby to think about. Keeping her healthy will be critical for its growth."

Jack shrugged. "Poor kid. I don't think it's been an easy go with her parents. She's been at boarding schools since she was seven and camps in the summer. The only interactions I've ever had with her were the occasional weekend visit and one vacation we took to St. John. I took my kids and Poppy and her mom a year ago over New Year's."

"Yes, she's mentioned that trip a number of times. Calls it the happiest week of her life."

Jack smiled. "That may have been because of the handsome young sailor she met on a charter. They had a bit of a whirlwind romance, which unfortunately ended when we came home."

She nodded. "Yes Danny. She talks about him a lot too."

He smiled. "I suspect Danny has whirlwind romances every week with a different young tourist."

"And yet she calls him the love of her life. This is what I mean about her fantasy life."

They talked awhile, then Liza suggested that they catch Poppy after yoga and find a quiet spot to talk. She excused herself, then returned a few minutes later. "All set. She'll meet us in the Atrium. Class is over in ten minutes, so we can head down now. I'll ask the kitchen to bring lemonades and water."

～

"So how are you, Poppy?" Jack leaned forward, elbows on knees. He sat in a straight-back chair about three feet from the love seat she'd flopped down upon. Liza sat off to the side, giving them space.

Poppy shrugged.

"Is there some way I can help?"

"Are you and Mom getting back together?"

"No, I'm sorry."

She crossed impossibly thin arms across an emaciated chest. "Why not?"

"We're not right for each other. Haven't been for a long time."

"That's not what she says."

Because she lives in a fricking dream world, he thought, gazing up at the therapist for support. "Well, it's what I say, and it's not going to change. I'm sorry."

Another shrug. "So I'm left with Wacko Mom and Waste-of-Time Dad."

"What about other relations or friends?"

"Yeah, like anyone's gonna want to have anything to do with a screwed-up mess like me."

"Well, we know that isn't true," Liza said, coming to sit beside her. "I asked Jack to come today to see if we could, the three of us, come up with a plan."

Jack took a deep breath. *Do not get involved. Do not get involved.* "What Liza's getting at...in terms of a plan...well, I...I'm sorry, but for the most part, I've got to back out, kiddo. It's too complicated with your mom right now, and it will only cause more upset."

"I know."

Surprised, he stared at her. "You do?"

She gave him a rueful smile. "Yup. I just needed to connect to someone sane and stable when I got here. You were the only person I could think of. No worries. I'll handle it."

He smiled, reaching forward to pat her knee. "Of course you will, kiddo. It's a long haul, I understand, but you're in a good place."

They talked awhile longer, then they took a walk around the

grounds. As they neared the main building, a bell sounded. "That's early dinner," Liza said. "What do you think, Poppy?"

Jack checked his watch. It was four thirty.

"Yeah, I'm ready." She turned to him. "You can go, Jack. No worries. Thanks for coming."

He opened his arms, and she stood still, staring at him as seconds went by. Finally, she stepped forward and allowed him to embrace her. She felt stiff, cold, and brittle as he wrapped his arms around her. *Poor kid*, he thought as she turned away and headed inside.

Liza walked him around to the front drive. "Thanks for coming. I know it was asking a lot."

"Glad I came. I doubt it changed anything, but it looks like she's got great support here. That's what's important. I'm sorry things aren't different. She's right, she needs someone sane and stable, but that someone can't be me except as a silent partner. Her father's got money, but please let Dr. Collier know that I'm happy to help with the costs if needed, anonymously, please."

"I will."

"Has she said much about the baby?"

"No. One day she says she's keeping it, the next, she wants to put her up for adoption."

"It's a girl, then?"

"Yes."

He shook his head. "What a mess." Poor kid, with Marsha as her grandmother.

"Yes...well, I've got a meeting, so I'll let you go." She extended her hand. "Safe trip."

As he headed into the city, he wondered if he'd done the right thing. He felt like a shit, but he hardly knew Poppy, and the thought of staying involved with Marsha in any way, shape, or form was unacceptable. *Hopefully, Barnum's Ledge, Lyddie's visit, and the Mystery Weekend will take my mind off all this*, he mused as he parked in the condo's underground garage.

~

Sandy had asked to keep Maisie for the night Wednesday as he and Pam wanted to take her to the circus. Alone again, Lolly thought as she headed out in the twilight for a beach walk. As she passed Osprey Cottage, going and coming, it was clear no one was home. Since Jack's SUV wasn't in the drive, she decided to walk out to the road, circle Netherfield, and come back down her driveway. As she reached the main drive, her mother's Mercedes came down the road.

Mavis braked and rolled down her window. "Hey, baby, what're you doing out in the dark?"

"Took a walk."

"By Jack's, I see. He's gone out of town for the night."

Of course he has. Off to be with his bimbo! "Good for him."

"Is something wrong, pet?"

"Nope."

"You like him, don't you?"

"Don't start, Mother."

"Hop in and come back to the house for a nightcap."

Nightcaps. Mavis's answer to all problems. "Thanks, but I'll pass. I'm tired, and we've got a big weekend ahead."

"We're looking forward to having my precious girl Friday night. Kendall and I have big plans. She can stay Saturday too."

"Thanks, but her dad's got her covered. He's got plans too. Night, Mom."

"Can I give you a lift? Coyotes have been howling the past few nights."

"Thanks, but I'll be fine," she said, waving her flashlight. "Night."

As she strolled down her driveway, she thought, *If it weren't for Maisie, I'd be fine being torn apart by coyotes right about now.*

CHAPTER 25

Lyddie arrived Thursday afternoon. Her father jumped up from his chair on the front porch where he'd been waiting and came down to greet her. "Hey, punky," he said, folding her into his arms. "Am I glad to see you."

She brushed strands of straight sandy hair from her forehead, eying him, her hazel eyes full of concern. "You okay, Dad?"

He grinned. "That obvious? It's been a rough week."

"What's happening?"

"Not now. I'll fill you in later. Let's get you settled and maybe we can take a walk?"

"Love it! Hey, this is a great little spot you got here."

"Isn't it? And wait till you see the jobsite."

After dropping her bags in the guest room, father and daughter headed out arm in arm for a beach walk. They strolled the shoreline in companionable silence, a gentle breeze blowing off the water, the cries of gulls surrounding them. Finally, they sat on a flat boulder Jack had already named Table Rock, and he gave her a quick rundown of his week with Marsha, Poppy, and the property. He decided not to mention Lolly Rogers for the time being.

When he'd completed his recap, Lyddie shook her head. "Dad,

when are you ever going to be free of that leech?" His kids had never liked Marsha, especially Lyddie.

"I'm trying, believe me."

"Sounds like Poppy's pretty messed up. Poor kid, with a mom like Marsha."

"She's in a good place right now," Jack said. "I hope she can get strong enough before she checks out."

"Meanwhile, how cool is this place?" she said, gazing out at the water. "I could definitely see living here. I could see *you* living here so I could visit."

"I'm thinking about it."

She turned to him, her eyes registering surprise. "Really? I was kidding."

"I'm not. I can work from anywhere, and it'd be great to get out of the city. Can't stay in the company condo forever."

"I can't believe you're deeding your condo to that witch."

"It's the easiest exit, believe me. Now no more talk about Marsha, Poppy, and the whole damn mess. I've made reservations at a great restaurant down the coast. Seafood's terrific."

She slipped off the rock. "I'm in, and I'm starving!"

"This fish is to die for," Lyddie said, waving her fork. She'd ordered the oven-roasted cod with littlenecks and chorizo served over risotto, kale, and butter beans.

"So's this," he said as he reached over and forked an olive from her plate. His plateful of tuna, house-made kimchee, grilled vegetables, tamari soy sauce, wasabi, and pickled ginger was already half gone.

In retaliation, she speared a perfectly grilled red pepper. "Mm, I should have gotten a side of the grilled vegetables."

"We can still put in an order."

She smiled. "I'm fine, Dad. So tell me about this mystery thing."

"It's being put on by two local women who run a cool book

company. They specialize in children's books, but they have a small line of mysteries in their catalog."

"What's the name of the company?"

"Merlin's Closet."

"I love that catalog!"

He nodded. "They're pretty successful, or so I understand."

"That's because they're really discerning. Every book they suggest is a great read. Lots of regional authors too."

Jack laughed. "You should give them a review. Your words would make great catalog copy."

"Do they have a shop here?"

"Nope, just a very crowded office. The weekend workshop's mostly taking place out at one of the women's homes. Lucy Morgan and her husband, Richard, have a huge farm, winery, and stables. Very cool. Wait'll you see it."

"Boy, in a short time, you've certainly gotten around," she said. "You sound like a local."

He grinned, enjoying the last few succulent bites of tuna. "Happy set of circumstances and chance meetings. This place makes you want to belong."

"That's good, right?"

"Yup, and guess what? Our closest neighbor is the other owner of Merlin's Closet, Lolly Rogers, so you'll be surrounded by local celebrities."

"Cool!"

On the drive home, he turned to her. "Hey, punky, I'm really glad you're here."

"Me too."

"And you don't mind if Jay comes down during the week? We'll probably hardly see him 'cause he's coming to paddleboard and surf. Maybe we'll have a meal or two?"

"Of course, I love Jay, you know that. Besides, I'm using this as my vacation after Mom's hovering in Maine. That wasn't relaxing at all! Who knows, I might be a local by the end of my stay."

"I can almost guarantee it!"

Lolly pulled up to Sandy and Pam's at noon Friday. "Here we are, sweet pea."

Maisie already had her seat belt popped. She hopped out and grabbed her pink rolling suitcase before Lolly could open her door. Why wouldn't Maisie be excited? Lolly's ex's home was a magical place, right on the river, crab nets and fishing poles always ready. The house had a simple design on the outside, but was incredible inside, with fifteen-foot ceilings, walls of glass, and exquisite furnishings. Pam's presence had softened the home, but it was still his in many ways.

"Hi, ladies!" Pam said as she swung open the front door.

"Hi, Pammy!" Maisie cried, ready to jump out of her skin, she was so excited. "Where's Daddy?"

Pam smiled at the child with genuine affection. "He's been working in the garden, so he was pretty dirty. He's just getting out of the shower."

"I'm going up and put this in my room," Maisie said, dragging her little suitcase up the stairs.

Pam turned to her. "Would you like something to drink?"

"Thanks, but I've got to run. I'm so grateful to you for having her all weekend. It's a huge help."

"We love having her. Always."

"I hear you three have big plans."

"Sure do. I hope the Mystery Weekend goes well."

"Me too. These things always sound great six months in advance, but doing them is always overwhelming."

"Fortunately, you've got the whole Event Central crew behind you. My dad loves nothing more than a good party. He's been reading mysteries nonstop for the past few months so he won't sound ignorant to all the mystery buffs."

Lolly laughed. "That's what Lucy said. And he doesn't even like mysteries, I hear."

"Oh no! He's a convert now."

"Well, gotta run. Have fun. Bye, sweet pea!" she called up the stairs.

"Bye, Mommy!"

She slipped out without seeing her gorgeous ex with tousled post-shower hair. There had been a time when Maisie had resisted staying with him, but not anymore, especially since Pam came on the scene. Lolly sighed, a pang of sadness washing over her. She liked Pam, and her rational maternal self was grateful and happy that Maisie was now with two people who loved her. Still, the pain of divorce never completely let go.

"Thank goodness Richard said yes to this," Lolly said as she and Lucy took one final survey of the tent, barn, and all the tables holding registration folders, books, and workshop materials. The buffet tables were inside the barn and other tables outside under the tent. "We could never have done it all without all these worker bees."

Hands on hips, Lucy nodded. "And thank goodness it's a nice evening too!"

Gail Morgan Miller and her husband, Tim, had been working with them all day, as had Wolfie and Weezie Morgan. Rich Morgan, the eldest son, and his fiancée, Karen Miller, Tim's sister had also arrived midday and pitched in. Weezie disappeared around one to teach two lessons down at the stables, but they spied her rounding the barn as they cleaned up.

"Porta-johns all installed," she called, heading for the house. "Dad's supervising."

Lucy waved to her stepdaughter, then turned back to Lolly. "He's been apoplectic all day wondering when they'd arrive."

"They did cut things a little close, if you ask me," Lolly said. "But they're here now, so that's all that matters."

"I think we're done. Shall we head in, clean up, and have a drink before the hordes descend?"

"Clean up, yes. Drink, no. I need my wits about me tonight and tomorrow," Lolly said, following her into the farmhouse. She'd put her change of clothes in one of the guest rooms. "See you in a few," she said.

Lucy stopped in the kitchen to chat with Callie. As Lolly ascended the stairs, she marveled, as she always did, at the beautiful home Richard Morgan had built after moving from Maine to Horseshoe Crab Cove. Comprised of nine bedrooms, each with its own bath, it had a sunporch that ran the length of the second floor. Only Richard and Lucy, her two teenagers, and Weezie lived there now, but the house was always filled during holidays and special occasions. Richard had eight children. Rich, the eldest, rented a house in town, but was planning to build a home with Karen either on Morgan's Fire land or at Land's End, the Miller family property at the south end of the peninsula. Ava and Dan owned a house in town, and Gail and Tim were building at Land's End. Two of Richard's sons lived out of town, Teddy in Providence, Rhode Island, Ben in Philadelphia, and Pam and Sandy were very happy in their home on the river.

Lolly stepped into the beautiful guest room, formerly Pam's bedroom, with its white cottage furnishings, and gazed longingly at the queen-sized bed and its beautiful quilt in soft blues and greens. *No time for a nap today,* she thought sadly. *A shower will have to do.*

CHAPTER 27

Weezie, Ava, and Gail manned the registration table as Lolly and Lucy mingled, greeting their guests. Richard and some of the stable hands were directing traffic and waving people to the parking area in one of the mowed, open fields. Wolfie and Rich were tending bar, and Karen Miller and Callie passed hot appetizers. There were tables scattered around the lawn, with cheese and crackers, vegetables, shrimp cocktail, and cold appetizer platters. Dan Fielding had filled a small dinghy with ice, and he and Tim had set up a raw bar where they were shucking oysters as guests strolled by.

"This is incredible, ladies," Frankie Brown said, greeting Lucy and Lolly. "You've outdone yourselves."

"Thanks, Frankie," Lucy said, hugging her mother's best friend. Frankie and Helen Winthrop, Lucy's mother, were members of the Darn Yarners, a group of eight local women who had known each other for years and had just recently celebrated their fortieth anniversary together. All the Yarners had signed up for Mystery Weekend along with a few of their husbands.

"Where's Mum?" Frankie asked, her sharp blue eyes twinkling with light. Dressed in her usual baggy khakis and muslin peasant blouse, the tall sixty-something exuded strength from her mop of wiry salt-and-pepper hair to her Birkenstock-clad feet. A painter, stained-glass artist like Lucy's mother, and a part-time private investigator, Frankie lived near Sandy and Pam on the river in a house that looked straight out of Middle Earth.

"She's around somewhere," Lolly said. "She arrived with Belle and Will. I think they were going to commandeer a Yarner table."

"That sounds like *your* mother's idea," Frankie said, winking.

"You know Mavis," Lolly said. Mavis was another Yarner, along with Tim's two aunts Grace and Hope and his mother, Faith. Rosa Rodriguez, Sandy's mother, was also a Yarner.

"Yes, I do. I see her directing traffic over there," Frankie said. "Excuse me, ladies."

As Frankie strolled off, Lolly gazed around, gasping as she spied a familiar face at the registration table. Surprised, Lucy turned to her. "You okay?"

"No, but I'll survive."

Lucy followed her gaze to where Jack stood chatting with Gail and Weezie, his arm around a slender young woman with sandy hair and a lovely smile who was shaking hands with the Morgan sisters. "There's Jack!"

"And his bimbo."

"She hardly looks like a bimbo."

"Young enough to be his daughter," Lolly said. "I'm going to check inside the barn." Before Lucy could utter another word, her partner disappeared. Shaking her head, she decided to say hello to Jack and his mystery women, aka George and Martha McDoogle.

As she approached Jack spied her and turned to his companion. "And here is one of the brains behind this operation! Lucy, come meet my daughter Lydia."

Lolly's words echoed as she came forward to greet the young woman. *Young enough to be his daughter.* Lucy stifled a laugh as she said, "So pleased to meet you, Martha McDoogle! Glad to have you back too, George."

Jack grinned. "Where's your partner in crime?"

"Oh, she's around somewhere," she said, thinking, *and I want to be there when she meets this bimbo!* She smiled at Lydia. "Are you here just for the weekend?"

"A whole week. Can't wait. It's really beautiful here."

"Yes, it is. We're very lucky. Please help yourselves to food and drink. Rich and Wolfie are manning the bar, and, as you can see, we have plenty of appetizers."

"I'll say," he said. "You all really know how to throw a party."

She laughed. "Mostly Richard's doing. He's never happier than when he's throwing some kind of event. Enjoy!"

As Jack and Lyddie wandered toward the bar, Lucy wondered if she should find Lolly and reveal the identity of Jack's date, but before she could decide, she was summoned to the kitchen. *Darn,* she thought. *I probably won't even see the big reveal after all.* "Coming!" she called to Callie.

～

"Is your mom here yet?" Hope Childs asked Lolly as the two strolled into the tent. "I've overbooked for next weekend, and I'm hoping she has room at the inn for a couple of my guests." Hope, another Darn Yarner, ran the Cove Yoga Center as well as Blueberry Lane B and B.

"She's here somewhere," Lolly said. "I don't think there's a wedding next weekend, but I know she's got people staying."

"I was thinking about Osprey Cottage."

"Unfortunately, it's rented to a long-term tenant."

"That's right. The ladies at yoga were buzzing about him."

"Speak of the devil," Lolly said as they approached the bar where Jack and his companion stood. At that moment, he turned.

"Oh, hi." Jack smiled at Lolly and her companion, a woman who appeared to be in her sixties, with snow-white shoulder-length hair and the lithe, toned body of a twenty-year-old.

"Hello." As Lolly greeted him, she noticed his companion was locked in rapt conversation with Wolfie. *Hmm...* She felt an elbow poke her side, so added, "Jack Faulkner, this is Hope Childs. She runs the local yoga studio and also one of two B and Bs in town."

"Hello, Mr. Faulkner," Hope said, coming forward to shake his hand. "Your reputation precedes you."

He grinned. "Uh-oh."

"All good, I assure you. I was just telling Loll that the gals at yoga had mentioned you."

He cringed. "Oh, boy. Good to know about your studio, though. My daughter Lyddie loves yoga. If I can manage to pull her away from the devilishly handsome winery manager, I'll introduce you." He winked. "She's suddenly taken a keen interest in fine wines."

Lolly stared at him. "Your daughter?"

He nodded, turning. "Hey, Lyd." She tore herself away from Wolfie and smiled at them. "Let me introduce the other genius behind today, Lolly Rogers, and this gorgeous lady, Hope Childs, runs the town yoga studio. Gals, this is my daughter Lydia."

She smiled, a smile so like her dad's, and stepped forward to shake their hands. "Hello, great to meet you both. I love yoga and am in heaven here. What a place. I can't wait to meet some of the authors tomorrow. I can't believe you have Patti Carroll tonight. I love her books."

Dumbfounded, Lolly felt rooted to the spot, unable to speak or move. Finally, as the three others chatted, she shook herself, spying her mother just outside the barn. When there was a lull in the conversation, she said, "Hope—there's Mom now. By the way, Frankie says you all are assembling a Darn Yarners table."

"Already on it, hon. Jack, Lydia, super meeting you. I'll expect you both at the studio. First class is always free."

As Hope headed for Mavis LaSalle and Lydia turned back to the bartender, Jack smiled, shrugging his shoulders. "Guess it's just you and me, babe. How are you?"

"Fine."

"This is an amazing event you and Lucy have staged. Really impressive."

"Many hands helped, including Richard, who's Mr. Party. He has large party planning down to a science. He built all this with social events in mind. That's his tent, and all the tables, chairs, bar, everything are owned by the farm. He opens Morgan's Fire to townspeople for all kinds of events. One of the most generous people I know."

Lolly was aware she was babbling, but she couldn't stop herself. Afraid of a conversational lull, she kept right on describing how the event had come together, who had helped, and what he could expect from tonight and tomorrow.

Jack listened attentively, a slight smile on his face.

Suddenly, the echo of a PA system interrupted, and she heard Lucy's voice. "Welcome, everyone. I can't see my partner in crime. Lolly, are you listening?"

"Oops, that's my cue," Lolly said, hurrying off, leaving Jack to admire her beautiful, perfect ass clad tonight in gray slacks that fit like a glove, and a white, jeweled T-shirt.

The evening ended around nine after Patti Carroll's after-dinner talk. The author of the Smoky River mystery series, Patti was amusing and witty, happily taking questions for almost forty-five minutes after her presentation. As guests trickled out, Jack found Lolly. "Great night. Looking forward to tomorrow."

Before Lolly knew what was happening, he leaned in for a hug that went on a bit longer than a friendly goodbye embrace. Breathless, she pushed away, her heart pounding, her body on fire.

He grinned. "I've missed that."

Me too, Lolly thought, but didn't dare speak. "Where's Martha?"

"Probably glued to Wolfie Morgan."

Lolly smiled as she scanned the dwindling crowd. She spied the young couple sitting on a bench near the house. "She does seem to be quite taken with him."

He nodded. "Never seen her like this with a guy. Gonna be hell to pay when I drag her away." His kind eyes regarded her and he looked as if he wanted to say more, and not about Lydia and Wolfie.

"Well, good night, then," she said. "I've got to help with cleanup."

His expression brightened. "We'd be happy to pitch in! I guarantee Lyddie will jump at the chance."

"Are you sure?"

"Of course. Give me a job."

"Why don't you check with Lucy or Richard? I'm going to check in the kitchen and see what Callie needs." She hurried off to forestall the urge to throw herself at him. The man was gorgeous. His presence made her feel wanton and sexy as no man ever had, not even her gorgeous ex. *I've been celibate way too long*, she mused, heading for the kitchen door.

CHAPTER 28

Saturday's events began with brunch at the farm, then a variety of workshops held around the property. As the partners stood together directing people to various locations, Lolly shook her head. "Thank goodness for good weather. So nice for people to be outside instead of stuck in the barns and the house."

Lucy nodded. "Where's your hunky Mr. McDoogle? Haven't seen him or his Martha all day."

"He's not my Mr. McDoogle, and they're in Patti's short story session."

"He is such a great guy. Richard's so excited to be working with him. Isn't it terrific that our men get along so well?"

"Would you stop!" Lolly whispered, elbowing her as two women approached to inquire about the location of the Murder Inc. session, given by Phil Chambers, a popular mystery writer who taught at Clifton College.

Lucy smiled. "That's in the house. If you head around to the front porch, the room is to the right just inside the door. Can't miss it." As the two women strolled off, she said, "Come on, Loll, you know you like him. What's stopping you?"

"Too handsome, too many entanglements, and the potential for serious heartbreak. Need I go on?"

"You hardly know anything about him. Isn't it worth giving him a chance?"

"Enough. I'm going to check out Phil's session."

CESAR AND ROSA OUTDID THEMSELVES WITH A SUMPTUOUS ITALIAN buffet served in the Grille's second-floor function room. The meal had guests oohing and aahing from start to finish. Trays of white and red lasagna, lobster, mushroom and cheese raviolis with several sauce options, and bowls of salad lined the buffet tables along one wall, and tables at the corners were covered with platters of antipasto, cheeses, and olives, as well as baskets piled high with warm crusty bread, flavored olive oils, and savory butters beside them. Dessert included an assortment of flans and tarts, bowls of gelato, and plates of fruit with chocolate dipping sauce.

As guests helped themselves to espresso and cappuccino, the Cherry Pickers began playing at the far end of the room, a small area for dancing in front of them. Since the participants were ninety percent women, friends and new acquaintances danced together, partnering up with whoever was nearby, or simply dancing solo to the rhythm of the popular local band. Lolly's sister, Marla, the lead singer, was in fine form as she belted out song after song.

As the partners watched the dancers, Lucy draped her arm on her friend's shoulder. "We did good. I think it's a success."

Lolly nodded. "Sure is, but I'm glad this is it and we didn't plan Sunday events. I'm pooped, and I've barely seen my daughter all week."

"The best part of tonight is that the Grille does all the cleanup."

"Hey, ladies, super job," author Phil Chambers said, jacket on his arm. "I'm heading home, but if you still want this old codger next year, give me a buzz." In his late seventies, he was still incredibly prolific, and all of his Cuttyhunk mysteries were bestsellers. Dapper in a checked sport shirt and gray slacks, he still had a full head of salt-

and-pepper hair, a neatly trimmed beard to match, and an eye for the ladies.

"Thanks, Phil," Lolly said. "We'll see you at next month's book signing, right?"

"You got it, doll!" He kissed and hugged them both, waving at various tables as he strolled toward the door.

"He's a charmer, isn't he?" Lucy said.

Lolly shook her head. "That's one word for it."

As Phil disappeared, the band began playing Van Morrison's "Have I Told You Lately," and Lucy sighed. "Oh, I love this song."

"And I love you," her husband said, slipping his arm around her waist. "Care to dance, baby?"

Lucy smiled, kissing him on the cheek. "I love you too, but as you can see, I'm conferring with my fellow event planner."

Lolly laughed. "Go on, you lovebirds! I'm fine." She watched the couple stroll off arm in arm and turn to begin their dance in perfect synchrony. *Will that ever be me?* Lucy looked beautiful in a simple linen sheath the color of ripe mangoes. Richard, fourteen years her senior, always gorgeous and well-dressed, wore a pale blue dress shirt and khakis.

"Dance with me?" Jack asked, stepping beside her with his hand extended.

Startled to find him beside her, she held out her hand and let him lead her to the crowded dance floor. As he pulled her close, he said, "You look lovely tonight."

She could feel her cheeks redden, powerless to stop her reaction. "You don't look so bad yourself." *Good enough to eat, in that faded green sport shirt and jeans.*

He pulled her even closer, his lips grazing her neck. "Finally," he whispered. Lolly felt his arousal tickling her tummy. Her instinct was to pull away, but instead, she gave herself to the music, melting into him, their bodies moving in delicious harmony.

Marla LaSalle noticed her sister's dance, and as the song ended, she announced, "Another slow one for the lovers."

As they began moving to strains of Etta James's "At Last," Lolly wondered if her legs might actually buckle if he let her go.

"You know," he whispered. "I'd make love to you right here and now if I could."

"When this dance ends, I'm wondering how you're going to explain that," she said gazing downward between them at the bulge in his jeans.

He grinned. "You're going to walk in front of me, very closely."

"We'll see about that," she said, resting her head on his strong, muscular shoulder. *At this moment, I'd walk with you to the ends of the earth, Jack Faulkner.*

CHAPTER 29

The song ended, the next a raucous band original celebrating love and life on the water. It seemed as if every person in the room was now packed on the small dance floor as Lolly and Jack slipped through the crowd toward the door. "Where are you leading me, you luscious, sexy woman?"

"You'll see," she said, all rational thought gone as she pulled him into one of the restaurant's store rooms and shut the door with her foot. "I'll probably regret this for the rest of my life," she murmured, voice husky and breathless as her arms circled his shoulders.

"I'll make sure you don't," he replied, capturing her lips in a deep, lingering kiss, his hands moving up and down the curve of her body, every touch like liquid fire.

As he found her breasts, caressing her through the thin cloth of her blouse, Lolly moaned, arching toward him, opening completely. "Oh, oh, oh."

His lips trailed kisses down her neck as his fingers deftly unbuttoned her blouse, then moved under lacy edges of her bra. He took one breast into his mouth, sucking and teasing her nipple to stiffness while caressing the other. "You have the most perfect breasts in the world," he whispered. Too lost to speak, Lolly lowered her hand and began to stroke him. "Okay, now you're trying to drive me crazy, babe. Not sure how long this old guy can hold on."

"Then don't," she said, boldly unzipping and releasing him. "Condom?"

"You're a wicked woman, sweetcakes. Two can play at this game." He reached under her skirt, slipping her panties down, his fingers delving into her wet depths as he found her clit and send her straight into orbit.

As her orgasm subsided, he gazed down, eyes soft in the light from outside street lamps. "Now I'm ready." He extracted a condom from his pocket and slipped it on as he settled back against the wall, pulling her to him, lifting her, wrapping her legs around him as he plunged into her, tentatively at first, allowing her to come to him, which she did in spades. Arms out straight, hands pressed against the wall behind him, Lolly rose and crashed against him again and again as if her very life depended on it.

Their feverish dance reached a blinding crescendo, and they collapsed against each other, drenched in sweat and each other. "Geez, baby, what the hell was that?" he whispered, kissing her shoulder and neck. For what seemed like hours, he held her, unwilling to break their sweet, intimate connection. Finally, he asked, "You okay?"

"Perfect, although I can't say the same for my clothes. How am I going to explain this mess?" she asked, holding up a corner of her wrinkly blouse.

"You're not. You're going to look like a woman who's been well fucked, and everyone will be jealous."

Shaking herself, Lolly felt like she was waking from a dream. "Seriously, Jack. This isn't funny."

"No, it isn't. I've just had the best sex of my life. Geez, baby, I feel like the luckiest man alive."

"Stop saying things like that and put me down," she said. She could feel him growing hard inside her, and every fiber of her being screamed, *again, again, again,* but voices in the hall pulled her back to reality. "Please?" she whispered, kissing him softly.

"Okay, but only because you asked me so nicely," he said, hands around her waist as he slipped out of her and set her down. As she groped around on the floor, he held something in front of her. "Looking for these?"

"Yes," she said, straightening and grabbing her panties. "How did you...?"

He grinned. "I put 'em in my pocket for safekeeping."

Fully dressed, her blouse buttoned, skirt smoothed as best she could, Lolly looked up at him in the dim light, her hand caressing his cheek. "This was probably a huge mistake, but I loved every minute."

"Me too. Thank you. Can we please make a plan to meet for dinner or something? I have so much I'd like to tell you."

"Let me spend a few days with Maisie, who I haven't seen all week, and then give me a call. You'll be busy, I'm sure, with your daughter visiting."

"Not that busy. I also suspect I'll see much less of her now that she's joined at the hip with a certain vintner."

"They are pretty chummy, aren't they?"

"Sure are, but not as chummy as us!" He drew her to him and kissed her deeply.

Lolly responded, wanting nothing more than to lose herself again. Finally shaking herself, she pulled back. "No more chumminess for now. I've got to get back to the party."

～

"Well, well, well," Lucy said, winking at her as she and Jack separated at the door.

Lolly turned bright red. "Well, well, nothing. Looks like people are thinning out. What needs doing?"

"The band just played their last song, so all we have to do is get our boxes of stuff to the car. Rosa says no rush, and we can leave them till tomorrow, if we want. Wolfie and Lydia just took a load to my car. Aren't you gonna tell me how your beautiful outfit ended up looking like it's been through a hurricane?"

"Ha-ha. Do I really look that bad?"

Lucy hugged her. "You look beautiful. You also look like you had fun, and that makes me deliriously happy."

"All right, Ms. Delirious. Let's get cracking."

A half hour later, almost everyone had departed. Jack and Lydia helped clean up, then prepared to depart. Lolly watched as Wolfie walked her out, Jack following behind. He turned back and waved, mouthing the words *I'll call you* as he mimicked holding up a phone.

She nodded, feeling her face turn bright red. *Whoa, boy!* she thought, turning away to find Lucy grinning behind her.

"Looks very promising, partner," she said.

Lolly grabbed her bag. "Ha-ha. Now let's go say goodnight to Rosa and Cesar. Mystery Weekend is officially over!"

CHAPTER 30

Sunday, Jack and Lyddie drove up the coast and parked at Sebring Park, then walked several miles along the Cliff Walk, the twenty-five mile pathway that bordered the ocean. At the three mile mark, they came to Sandy's.

"Wow, "Lyddie exclaimed, gazing up at the huge rambling structure that jutted out over the cliffs, the ocean crashing beneath it.

Her father whistled. "So that's the place."

"What is it?"

"According to local gossip, it's the most successful music venue in New England. It's called Sandy's, the name of its former owner."

"Pam's Sandy?"

"The very one."

"Why'd he sell if it's so successful?"

"Wanted new challenges, I expect. The property sold for many millions, so that might have been an incentive. Apparently, Cady Promotions, the new owners, approached him."

"Well, that'll help bankroll the new restaurant, huh?"

"Yup."

"People have a lot of money around here, don't they?"

Jack chuckled. "Not everyone. Richard Morgan is in a class by himself, and Sandy made out well with this, but the rest of us are just slogging along."

"Yeah, right, Dad, you're really eking out a living in your pristine little antiques-filled cottage on Mavis's estate."

"There are degrees of slogging, oh innocent child."

"Uh-huh." They had paused in the shadow of Sandy's, and she stood facing him, hands on hips. "So are we ever gonna talk about the elephant in the room?"

"What's that supposed to mean?" he asked, knowing full well what she meant.

"You and Ms. Rogers? I can see you guys are gaga over each other."

Jack grinned. "Gaga? Hmm...maybe not the word I'd use."

"Then what? How should I describe two people who disappear in the middle of an event that one of them is running and return looking like they'd taken more than one roll in the hay? I mean, Dad—really? Everyone knew what you'd been doing in that storeroom."

"Yeah?"

"Yes!"

"Well, what about you and the handsome Mr. Morgan?"

"Did you see us come out of a storeroom half-dressed? I don't think so! Besides, never mind that. We're talking about you." She pointed her finger, poking his chest.

Another grin. "What can I say? I like her."

"More than like her?"

"Maybe. We're takin' it slow."

"Yeah, right. If last night was takin' it slow, I hate to think what full speed ahead would look like."

Jack laughed. "Well, in my mind, I'm takin' it slow, after Marsha and all." They had turned back and were now walking southward toward Sebring Park and the car.

"How is the wicked witch anyway?"

"Same."

"You're not still seeing her, are you?"

"Poppy got in a bit of trouble. I dropped her at her mother's, that's all."

"When's she going to move out and disappear?"

"I'm giving her the condo." He cringed, waiting for her explosion.

Lyddie didn't disappoint. "Dad! How could you? She's been a money-grubbing leech from day one."

He shrugged. "This is it. No more after this."

"What about Poppy?"

"I may be helping out a little there. Just till she gets back on her feet."

"Doormat."

"Maybe."

Lyddie paused, reaching over to squeeze his shoulder. "Sorry, I didn't mean that."

"Yes, you did, and it's true."

"This may not be the best time to bring this up, but Mom's dating again. Mitch. He's some venture capitalist she met in New York when she was staying with Aunt Peggy."

"Good for her. Nice guy?"

"If you like stuck-up narcissists. You should see the gifts he buys her. Diamond bracelets, gazillion-dollar clothes. He's kind of a women's clothes freak, if you ask me."

"Does your mom seem happy?"

Lyddie shrugged, gazing out to sea. "I guess."

"Well then, that's all that matters."

"Okay then, back to you and Lolly!"

"Oh, no, you don't. My turn to give you the third degree about your wolfman."

"Look at this mess!" Lucy cried as they gazed around their office, floor-to-ceiling boxes, stacks of unpacked books, and every table and desk piled with a mountain of papers and files.

"As I've said a million times, we need an assistant." Lolly ran a box cutter across the top of a box. "Someone who can take over as office manager, make sense of the paperwork, and take orders. All the stuff that we say we're going to do next week and never do."

"Andy does that," her partner said, referring to Andy Roby, the accountant who handled their taxes.

Lolly shook her head. "No, he doesn't. I wonder if Lynn might be interested?"

"Good idea. I'll ask her. Now before we get into today's chores, let's sit with our coffees, and you can tell me all about Mr. Dreamy."

"Nothing to tell."

Lucy flopped down on the floor cross-legged and toasted with her large mocha latte. "Oh, yes, there is! Richard's dying to know too!"

"Oh, terrific." Lolly threw up her hands. "Well, as long as we keep your husband in the know! Why don't we put an announcement in the *Cove Gazette*?"

Lucy clapped her hands. "Great idea! Now, seriously, sweetie. This is major."

"This is when I scream for help!" Lolly said, flopping down beside her, back against the wall. "This is not me! Half the town knows I slipped off in the middle of dinner to screw around with Jack Faulkner in the storeroom."

Lucy smiled, patting her knee. "Not half the town. Just a few of us, and we love you and are happy for you."

"It's mortifying."

"Love is messy."

"Easy for you to say when you're happily married to Mr. Perfect."

"He is pretty perfect most of the time, but don't forget, we had a mortifying moment of our own witnessed by almost his entire family."

Lolly laughed. "Ah, yes, the infamous bump and grind in his office? But that's you two, not me. Besides, look how incredible your life is now."

"Yes, but as you may recall, it took a long while and a lot of work before some members of his family forgave me and us."

"Would you do it again?"

"Absolutely."

Lolly turned to her, smiling. "Me too. Now let's get to work, or this will take all day, and I'm picking Maisie up at three."

"So no more details?"

"Absolutely not."

Lucy set down her coffee and grabbed the box cutter. "Spoilsport." As she ran the knife over a box, she said, "And you're right. I'll call Lynn and beg her to join us today."

CHAPTER 31

Jack had pushed hard for an expedited closing on Barnum's Ledge, and he got it. Compass would take possession in two weeks. In the meantime, Sam Morgan had drawn up plans, and orders were placed for lumber, fixtures and materials. Jack had convinced Roland that they should reserve a company unit with a two-year option for him to buy it. Tuesday morning, his boss drove down to Horseshoe Crab Cove to walk the property and explore the village. He came away impressed. As Jack walked him to the car late in the afternoon, Roland said, "That's a talented architect you're working with."

"Sure is. One of the best in the country right now."

"I'm sure he's a hot commodity, but send me his contact info. I'd love to hire him for a couple of upcoming projects."

"You're right. He's hot right now and trying to focus on single dwelling properties. I only lured him to this through his uncle."

"Ah, yes, Richard Morgan's reputation and reach are considerable."

"He's a great guy."

"Met him once years ago, overseas, actually. His mind was going a mile a minute."

Jack chuckled. "That sounds like Richard. We should have lunch if you come down again. I know he'd love to show you around the farm and winery."

"Good stuff. Well, buddy, I'd better get going. You're doing great work here. Careful that what you build doesn't destroy what's special about this place. I've made a lot of money in this business. Enough to know that places like this are an endangered species."

"I hear you," Jack said, waving as Roland's driver opened the car's back door. After the Escalade disappeared, he walked back to chat with Pete Santoro for a few minutes, then headed to the cottage. He drove in and parked next to Jay Hallowell's Jaguar. He spied his friend and daughter chatting on the back porch, so he grabbed a beer and headed out to join them.

"Hey, buddy," Jay said, standing and shaking his hand. "Nice little crib you've got here."

Athletic and toned, his friend had the wiry build of the marathon runner he was. Prematurely bald, his sharp, angular features had intimidated many an opponent in the courtroom, even as his arresting brown eyes sparkled with mischief. Jack always said he never wanted to be on the wrong side of Attorney Hallowell for good reason. Jay rarely lost.

He grinned. "A rental crib."

"This is some property. Can't wait to see *your* project."

"Oh, you will. I thought we'd take the grand tour tomorrow morning, then spend the rest of the day on the beach watching you wipe out."

"Ha-ha, you wish. I've been practicing. They have one of those surf machines at my gym now. I'm gonna hang ten and show you how it's done, big daddy. I'm so confident, I didn't even bring the paddleboard."

"Is your tour going to include Morgan's Fire?" Lyddie asked, failing miserably in her effort to sound nonchalant.

Jack smiled. "Yup, and the village too. And it's *our* tour, punky. I assume you want to come with us?"

"Great, sure. Of course!"

Jay watched the interchange with sharp eagle eyes that seldom missed a nuance or gesture. "Okay, okay... What's going on here? What am I missing?"

Lyddie shot out of her seat. "Nothing! Anyone want another beer? I've got some emails to write."

As she disappeared into the house, not waiting for them to reply about the beers, Jay turned to him. "Did I touch a nerve?"

"My daughter's in love," Jack whispered.

"Our little Lyddie?"

"Yup, and she's not so little anymore. I fear the object of her adoration may be proving elusive."

"Where is he? Do we need to give him a beating?"

"He manages the winery at Morgan's Fire. Wait'll you see that place. It's the vision of kazillionaire Richard Morgan. Amazing property. I've been asked to consult about a small farm-to-table restaurant near the vineyard."

"Love those places. This should be interesting."

"Yup."

"So what's new with you? I hear you have a little something going yourself."

"Maybe. She's a local bookseller. Mavis LaSalle's daughter. Lives right here on the property. Next door, in fact. Have you checked in to your room at Netherfield yet?"

"Nope. I thought I'd check in with you guys first. Does this daughter have name?"

"Lolly. Lolly Rogers."

"You're kidding—Lolly? Like Lollipop? That has possibilities."

"Ha-ha. She's pretty great, actually. You may run into her around the property. She's got an adorable seven-year-old, Maisie."

"Uh-huh. You're being cautious, I hope? You barely extricated yourself from the Blake fiasco."

Jack leaned back, rubbing his eyes. "Do I want to hear how that's going?"

"She signed the papers. The condo's hers. I had the guys pack up your things. They're in a storage unit. I've been waiting to talk to you about the daughter's mess. How much are you willing to shell out there? It could end up being a black hole. Sounds like the kid's pretty messed up."

"Happy to help as long as the money's put in a managed trust so neither she nor her mother can get to it."

"Are we talking twenty grand or...?"

"Earmark a hundred, put it in a trust, and when that's gone, they're on their own. Her dad's got money. Let him take over after that."

"Are you crazy, man? That's way too much for a relationship that never should have happened in the first place."

"It's not Poppy's fault. I'd like to help her get straightened out if I can."

"Farrell Park'll take most of it. That place is ridiculously overpriced for what they do."

"Maybe, but if she gets healthy, it's worth it."

"You are officially my worst client ever."

"Let's talk about something else, okay?" Jack closed his eyes, suddenly weary and wishing he could take a nap.

Jay gazed out at the backyard, spying two figures emerge from the woods. "Like who is that gorgeous babe and her tiny elf friend. Could it be the beautiful Lolly?"

Eyes wide open now, Jack stood and waved as mother and child crossed the lawn.

"Hi, Jack!" Maisie called, jumping up and down, both arms waving. Her mother raised her hand as she urged the child along, clearly not intending to stop and chat.

Too late. The men were off the porch and headed their way. "Hi, ladies," Jack called. "Want to stop for a drink?"

"Thanks, but we're headed for a quick beach walk, then supper at the big house," Lolly said, gazing from him to his companion.

"Lolly and Maisie, this is my friend, Jay Hallowell. Jay, Lolly and Maisie Rogers."

"I'm Rodriguez," Maisie said, skipping forward to shake Jay's hand. "Mommy's Rogers, and I have my daddy's last name."

"Well, pleased to meet you, Maisie Rodriguez, and your beautiful mother, Ms. Rogers."

Lolly put her hands on Maisie's shoulders. "Yes, well, great to meet you, Jay. Jack...Thanks, for the invitation, but we've got to move along."

As they hurried off, disappearing into the woods on the opposite side of the lawn, Jack said, "Did I mention she's kind of like a deer in the headlights, gun-shy, terrified, and a host of other things?"

"Nope, but she's hot. What a babe."

Jack laughed. "You don't know the half of it. Now come on. Let's get you settled at the big house, and then we'll head to dinner. There's a great seafood place down the coast."

"I'm in!" Jay said, grinning from ear to ear as he followed him.

CHAPTER 32

Maisie in bed sound asleep, Lolly brought the newest Louise Penny mystery to her favorite chair in the den, soft music playing in the background. Much as she loved the author, all she could see when she stared at the page was Jack's blue eyes. *Impossible!* she thought, setting the book aside and closing her eyes. The phone's ring startled her.

"Hey, Loll!" a familiar voice said.

"Jen, is that you?" She recognized the voice of her dear friend and her mother's ward, Jen Honeywell. Mavis had taken Jen and her brother Jerry in after their parents' death, and the two women had spent their high school years together.

"It is. How are you?"

"Fine. Busy, crazy, the usual. How about you?"

"Okay."

"You don't sound okay. Have you talked to Mom?"

"Not yet. I wanted to check in with you first. See if you'll be around. I was thinking of coming for a couple of days. I'll stay with her, but I'd rather hang out with you and Maisie."

"Of course. You're catching me at a good time. Merlin's Closet just ran a mystery weekend, so Lucy and I are sort of taking a few weeks off to decompress before tackling the mess that is our office and business."

"Great. I'll call Mom and plan to come down Friday, for the weekend."

"What's up? You sound kind of down."

"I'll fill you in when I see you. I'll just leave you with two words—Rip Lassitor."

"Wow, Rip Lassitor, that's a blast from the past," she said, referring to a former classmate who had been the secret heartthrob of every girl in high school.

"Not anymore. He's about to become my new boss."

"Really?"

"Yup."

"You don't sound happy about it. I'd rather be under him than most men, if you get my meaning."

"I do, and it's not funny. Anyway, more soon! And I want to catch up on all your news, love life and all."

Lolly cringed, then smiled. *It might be really helpful to talk through the craziness with Jack with Jen. Sensible, down-to-earth Jen,* she thought. "Can't wait to see you!"

As they followed Richard Morgan down to the stables, Jack spied Lolly and Lucy working in the barn and waved. Their host noticed his gaze and said, "Last bits of cleanup from Mystery Weekend. I offered to help, but they shooed me away." Both women waved back, then returned to their work.

"Sounds like that was quite an event," Jay said.

"Sure was. My wife and her partner are extraordinary. We'll stop by and say hello at the end of our tour." Grinning from ear to ear, Richard sallied forward. When Jack had phoned, their host had gladly cleared his morning to show them around the farm. "We're delighted to have your buddy in town for a while. His input on the restaurant has already been really helpful."

Jay nodded. "He's quite a guy."

"What a beautiful horse!" Lyddie cried as they neared the corrals. A sandy-haired man in jeans and T-shirt stood beside a sleek black giant, talking softly.

"That's Tornado, one of the first mustangs we acquired. Still pretty wild even now after almost two years, but we love him." He pointed to man and horse. "Our head trainer, Gus, is the only one who can go near him, although my daughter Weezie is almost there. Gus, come meet our friends!" he called.

They had just started chatting with Gus when a petite young woman emerged from the barn, leading a stocky white horse with brown-and-white spots. She wore her dark brown hair cut short in a stylish pixie, and her chocolate eyes danced with light. In jeans and the same kind of T-shirt as the trainer, as she neared them. Jack read, "Morgan's Fire" splayed across her blue shirt, above it, a beautiful image of sunrise over the water. "Hey, Dad, Jack, Lyddie. Good to see you!"

"Great logo," Jack said. "Who does your PR?"

She posed, then did a mock curtsy as both men stared at her chest. "My sister Gail."

"Weezie, this is my friend, Jay Hallowell."

"Pleased to meet you, Ms. Morgan."

"And you and your interest in our logo," she said, eyes shining with mischief.

Richard watched his daughter, always an inveterate flirt. "We have a great graphic designer who does all our artwork. She's created signs, labels for the winery, you name it. Incredibly talented gal."

"I'd love her contact info," Jack said to their host, as Gus excused himself and headed into the barn.

"You bet. She's based in Maine, but after visiting here a couple of times, she's considering a move south. This place does that to people. Draws you back like a magnet."

"And who's this handsome steed?" Jay asked, stepping closer to pet the horse's nose.

"Crackers. He's one of our stable horses," Weezie said, as she petted his muzzle.

"American Paint?"

"Yup. Are you a rider?"

"When I get the chance," Jay said, coming to the horse's other side, patting his withers.

"You're welcome to come riding while you're here."

"Thanks," he said, "but surfing's won out today, and I have to head back tomorrow."

"There's always next time," Weezie said. Grabbing the horse's lead, she strolled off.

Lyddie, Jack, and her father had been quietly observing the interchange. Finally, Richard stepped forward. "That's our Weezie for you. Runs all the pony camps, riding lessons, and what have you. I've been trying to get her back to college, but she's got a mind of her own, I'm afraid. And here's our resident vet," he said, waving to a lovely ash-blonde with a large woven bag slung over her arm who appeared from behind the barn. As she passed Weezie, the two women appeared to ignore each other.

"Hiya," she said, approaching. "Just checked Nellie's foal. She's doing well. Mama too."

"Great."

"You haven't named her yet?"

"That's Weezie's department," Richard said. "Did you ask her?"

The woman raised an eyebrow. "I'll let you nag your daughter about that one."

"These are friends of ours, Jack and Lyddie Faulkner and Jay Hallowell. I'm giving them a tour of the farm. Jack, Lyddie, Jay, this is Dr. Kiki Bloom."

After hearing about the wild horse rescue program from Kiki and Gus Casey, the group toured the stables, then decided to walk to the winery. They climbed the rise behind the stables to Laura's Bench, a memorial to Richard's first wife that he had brought from their previous home in Maine. On a grassy knoll overlooking the farm below, the river to the east, and fields to the north and west, the teak bench with its small brass plaque afforded some of the most spectacular views on the peninsula.

"Wow, what a spot," Jay said as they gazed around.

Richard nodded. "My first wife, Laura, loved the open fields, so we brought her here. She'd have loved this view."

As they headed north along the path that followed the cliffs, they spied a lone figure approaching. As soon as she saw him, Lyddie's eyes lit up. "There's Wolfie."

Richard waved to his son, winking at Jack over her head. As she quickened her pace, leaving the three men behind, he whispered, "So, do I detect a spark?"

"More like a forest fire, I suspect," Jack said under his breath.

"Ah, to be young and in love," Jay said. The three chuckled, watching the young people greet each other ahead of them.

"THIS IS A GREAT SPOT, BUT MY SURFING'S A LITTLE RUSTY," JAY SAID AS he leaned back in his canvas chair. On this warm summer day, Moonstone Beach was almost deserted. "Wonder where Mavis got these chairs? They're the most comfortable beach chairs I've ever sat in."

"I suspect our hostess spares no expense for her high-paying clients' comfort," Jack said, stretching out.

"You know, buddy, I was teasing you about being out in the middle of nowhere, but this sleepy little town might have possibilities after all."

Jack grinned, exchanging glances with Lyddie. "Uh-huh. Your changed perspective wouldn't have anything to do with the bevy of beauties you've been flirting with all day, would it?"

"You gotta admit that doc is hot, and wouldn't I like to go riding with Dick's daughter? She's a babe."

"Don't forget the comely Cara," Jack said, referring to the vintner's assistant, Cara Feldspar. Of the three women, she seemed the least interested in Jack's handsome friend.

"That would be wrong forgetting that blue-eyed goddess in blue jeans. She should be on the wine labels."

"Yuck," Lyddie said, pulling out her book.

Jay grinned, sitting up and winking at Jack. "Okay, change of subject. What do we know about the dark, brooding wolfman who has captured a certain young lady's heart?"

"Good grief," she said, closing her book and standing up. "I'm going for a walk."

"You shouldn't tease her," Jack said. "Lyd's never been able to take teasing or meddling in her affairs."

"Affairs. Now, I like the sound of that."

"You know what I mean."

"And speaking of affairs, anything new with the fair Lolanda?"

"We're having dinner tomorrow night. Lyddie's going out with her wolfman, and Maisie is with her dad."

"Sure you're not taking on more baggage, buddy? I mean, the woman's a knockout, but with a kid and all?"

"It's dinner."

"Yeah, right. I see the way you look at her, man. I know you, remember?"

Jack turned away, gazing out to sea. "Looks like the surf's picking up. You gonna give it another go?"

"Why not?" Jay said, grabbing his board.

Am I taking on more baggage? he thought, watching his friend paddle out over the rolling waves. *Lolly's not Marsha, but maybe we've rushed into something for which neither of us is ready.*

CHAPTER 33

"Have fun, you two," Jack said as Lyddie and Wolfie departed. She looked lovely in a white summer dress, a shawl draped over her shoulders. Wolfie's expression when he saw her reinforced his baby's status as a woman, a grown-up woman who men like Wolfie Morgan desired. *Definitely not my little punky anymore.*

He followed the couple out, then hopped in the SUV and drove out to pick up Lolly. On the front porch, she stood as she spied his car. She wore a sleeveless, knee-length dress cinched at the waist with a skirt that swished. Its floral fabric offset her beautiful coloring, and the V-neck afforded a tantalizing view of that glorious cleavage. A daring choice for a full-figured woman, it suited her perfectly. Her lustrous hair fell in waves over her shoulders, a cream-colored cashmere shawl draped over one arm. She wore strappy summer sandals with five-inch heels. *And oh those legs!*

He jumped out and came to greet her. "You look sensational."

Lolly blushed, pleased that the dress her mother had helped her choose on a weekend in New York City had the effect she'd hoped. She felt wanton and sexy, at the same time praying she wouldn't trip and fall in her crazy high heels.

"Thanks, you don't look too shabby yourself." Gorgeous as always in a casual beige linen summer suit, he wore a blue shirt and gaily patterned tie that accentuated his blue eyes, even from a distance. He opened her door, and she slipped by him.

As they drove out of the estate, she asked, "Where are we going? I hope I'm dressed appropriately?"

"You're perfect. I made a reservation at Ballard's. Is that okay? I keep hearing about it and haven't tried it yet."

"It's great. It's Lucy and Richard's favorite restaurant."

"But not yours?"

She smiled, gazing straight ahead. "It's kind of a romantic spot, and I can't say as I've had many romantic encounters since moving here."

He smiled, giving her a quick glance. "Well then, maybe we can change that tonight. With you in that dress, how could it not turn into a romantic encounter?"

PERCHED AT THE EDGE OF THE SEA, BALLARD'S WAS OWNED BY FIVE-STAR chef Andre Cleves, who employed a legion of assistant cooks and a talented manager, Jock Farraday, who had designed and now ran the restaurant. Through creative marketing and an eye for exquisite interior design, Jock had succeeded in attracting legions of loyal regulars. The restaurant was located in the wealthy town of Leeside, about ten miles north of the village, and foodies traveled many miles to enjoy Andre's ever-changing, imaginative menu.

"I can see why Richard loves this place," Jack said, as they scanned the menus Peter, their waiter, had handed them as he disappeared to get their drinks.

"Pricey, you mean?"

"No, inventive. You don't see selections like this in many places. It may bode well for their farm-to-table operation."

"I hope so," she said, acutely aware of his knee as it brushed hers under the table. "Of course, they won't have Andre."

"From what I've seen and heard so far, I'd be willing to bet they'll find some high-powered chef and lure him or her here with a salary and benefits they can't refuse. Richard and his son-in-law have pretty deep pockets."

"Bottomless," she said, gazing up and smiling. "They've both been incredibly generous to the village. Mom too, on a slightly smaller scale."

"Your mother's no slouch either, is she?"

Lolly shrugged, rubbing her leg against his. "Mavis is Mavis."

Jack leaned across the table, a mischievous grin on his face. "You know, if you keep doing that with your leg, I'm gonna have come over there on that comfortable bench and ravish you before Pete returns with our drinks."

Lolly could feel heat crawling up her neck. Even her chest was red with her blushing. "Me? You're the one who's been playing footsie!"

He laughed. "Footsie? I know a bit about footsie, babe. This is way beyond footsie."

Lolly moved her legs sideways as Peter appeared with her gin and tonic and his scotch. She looked up at the waiter and said, "Peter, would it be okay if we moved the table out a few inches? I'm a little cramped."

"Of course! Allow me."

Jack stood, grinning as he helped Peter lift the heavy marble-topped table. "Thanks," he said as he took his seat.

"Are you folks ready to order, or shall I give you more time?" They asked for fifteen minutes, and he disappeared.

"Very smooth there with Pete," he said, clinking her glass with his own. "What shall we drink to?"

"A beautiful view," she replied, quickly looking away from those blue eyes to gaze out at the sea. *One of the best tables in the restaurant. I wonder how he managed this?* As their legs were no longer touching, her heart rate was gradually returning to normal.

"It is, but I was thinking of something a bit more personal. Maybe something about us?"

She reached over and clinked his glass. "To new friends, then."

"To new friends who are incredibly sexy and beautiful."

"And too charming for their own good," she added, meeting his eyes.

"Have I told you how much I love your beautiful eyes?"

"Several times," she said drolly.

"I had planned to suggest that we take things slower tonight—since we've just met and all—but after seeing you in that dress, those crazy thoughts are gone."

"That's just lust talking. Besides my eyes, what else would you like to talk about?"

"I don't know, really. All I know is I'm really interested in you, Lolly. Very fond of you, actually, which is kind of disconcerting given that we just met."

"And how does that relate to the taking-it-slow part?"

"My life's kind of a mess right now with the whole Marsha thing and her daughter. I mean, they're not in my life anymore, but I'm supporting Poppy's treatment."

"Oh?"

At that minute, Peter appeared, and they ordered. Jack chose lobster rossejat, described as lobster, toasty pasta, and plenty of rich aioli. Lolly selected lobster gnocchi, her favorite summer pasta dish. They decided to share a warm beet, goat cheese, and arugula salad. "Very good choices," Peter said, bowing as he took their menus. "Can I interest you in an appetizer? Our local oysters are superb right now."

"Perfect," Jack said. "We'll share an order."

"Of course," the short, trim waiter said, bowing again before hurrying off.

Suddenly, Jack looked stricken. "Shit, I'm sorry," he said, gazing at her. "I didn't even ask you what you wanted or if you like oysters. What a clumsy oaf."

She smiled, reaching over and taking his hand without thinking. "It's fine. I love oysters. I'm not a big appetizer person, but I'll be happy to have a couple."

His fingers stroked her palm, sending shivers through her. "Good. All I could think about was oysters, aphrodisiac. Gotta have 'em."

As if we need an aphrodisiac, she thought, withdrawing her hand. "So back to our taking-it-slow conversation. How do oysters fit into that?"

Chuckling, he leaned back in his chair. Well now, let me tell you all about that."

THEY SPENT THE MEAL CHATTING ABOUT LIFE—PAST AND PRESENT— and enjoying food that Jack pronounced to be some of the best he'd ever tasted. They shared an order of mini pavlovas with their coffee, then Lolly excused herself to go to the ladies' room with the words, "I'm happy to split the check, so please wait until I return."

Once in the bathroom, she stared at her reflection, reapplying lipstick and freshening her blush. *What do I want here?* she thought. *How do I want this evening to go?* Since no answers came, she returned to the table resolved to let the evening unfold as it would. Predictably, Jack had settled up with Peter and waved away her attempts to contribute.

"I've got an idea," he said as they strolled to the door, waving to Peter on their way out.

"Oh?"

"What do you think about a walk along the seawall?"

"I'd love it, but not in these shoes. Let me throw them and my purse in the car. I don't suppose you'd have a sweatshirt or extra jacket in there, would you?"

"Might have, let me check. You can always use my jacket too."

He grabbed her shoes and purse, and Lolly waited on the walkway to avoid the lot's blanket of clamshells. When he returned, he had a windbreaker slung over one shoulder. "Want this now?"

"No, I'm fine with my wrap. Maybe if the wind kicks up."

It was a short walk across the parking lot to the smooth, cement seawall. After watching her pussy-footing with each step, he said, "That's it. Allow me," and swept her into his arms, carrying her the short distance.

As he set her down, holding her close for longer than necessary, she said, "Thank you, but that really wasn't necessary."

He grinned. "Yeah, but it was fun, wasn't it?"

They walked hand in hand along the smooth, recently repaved seawall. As the wind kicked up, she shivered. "Here," he said, removing his jacket and draping it over her shoulders.

"Thanks," she said, momentarily leaning into him, head on his shoulder, then pulling back.

"You okay?"

"Yes, just wondering what we're doing."

"Enjoying a beautiful walk together."

"Yes, there's that. It's just a bit overwhelming at times. Confusing, scary, crazy."

They had reached the archway leading to the Cliff Walk. As they passed through the craggy stone doorway, they could see the outline of Sandy's several miles ahead. In the shelter of the arches, he pulled her closer, leaning back against the rock face. "It doesn't have to be any of those things."

"Says you."

"Because it's true. I'm attracted to you, Lolly, very attracted, obviously. I really like spending time with you and want to continue seeing you. How can I make it comfortable and less scary for you? What do you need?"

Tears welled in her eyes, and she gazed up at him in the growing twilight. "That's the trouble. I don't know what I need. All I know is what I don't need—to be hurt again. I don't even blame Sandy. If I'm telling the truth, I was a full participant in our marriage breakup. His infidelities came long after I'd already checked out."

"Divorce is never simple, and it's seldom only one person's fault."

"What happened with you and Lyddie's mom?"

Where'd that come from? he thought, giving her a quizzical look.

Before he could answer, she shook her head. "Sorry, so sorry. None of my business."

He moved his hands to rest on her waist, holding her gently. "Well, I think I told you Cynthia and I married young. We had the kids, boom, boom, then life became a blur. I was working all the time. She got into a bunch of volunteering. Her family comes from money, so philanthropy is in her DNA. She was helping to manage a big family trust when she met Derek, not the first of her many conquests, as it turned out.

"We tried to make it work, went to marriage counselling, all the things you do, but truth is, we weren't right for each other. We hung on a while for the kids. Then she announced that she wanted to divorce so she could marry Derek, Dr. Derek. He's a cardiologist in Portland. Moved there at Cynthia's request so they could live in the family compound. It's a pretty cool place, actually. Cynthia and Dr. Derek lasted five years."

"I'm sorry. That must have been painful."

He shrugged. "I was pretty worked up at the time, but I've mellowed. Years of yoga, meditation, and mindfulness, not to mention a great therapist, helped me let go of the anger. You wouldn't have liked me back then. I had quite a temper." As she traced the line of his jaw with her fingertip, he reached up and took her hand. "The last thing I want to do is hurt, scare, or confuse you, babe, never mind drive you insane. I just like being with you. We can stay friends, if you like. Take things slow." He grinned, turning her hand and kissing her palm. "I can exercise self-control when necessary."

She moved closer, pressing against him. "What if I can't?"

"Well, that could be...what could it be?" he whispered as her lips found his and her arms circled his neck.

His fingers gently slipped under her dress's V-neck. He trailed kisses down her neck to her chest, burying his face in her, tongue licking as he peeled back her lacy bra, releasing her breast, taking her in his mouth. Lolly moaned, arching against him, his arousal obvious as she moved rubbing up and around with increasing urgency.

"Oh, babe, you are killing me. You know that, don't you?" he whispered as his hand move downward, lifting her skirt and slipping her panties down to find her warm, wet depths. As he found her clit, Lolly cried out, "Oh," all thought obliterated by a crescendo of sensation as he brought her to a spectacular orgasm.

As he kissed her deeply, tongues entwined, their bodies ached for each other. She moved her hand down to caress and stroke him, fingers finding his fly as she unzipped and released him, his size startling as always. Somehow, he extracted a condom from his back pocket and sheathed himself.

"You ready, baby?" he asked, his voice gruff with desire.

Unable to speak, Lolly nodded, and he reached around and grabbed her ass, lifting her as he slipped a condom on and plummeted into her depths. Tentative at first, he gradually went deeper and deeper as she opened up to take him, arching and thrusting to meet his every move.

Blinded by passion, Lolly left confusion and fear behind as they moved to an explosive crescendo of sensation and release. They collapsed against each other, Jack's back against the rocks, her legs hugging his waist. He kissed her neck, then found her lips for a long, lingering kiss. When he pulled back, scanning their surroundings for possible passersby, he whispered, "You are the most amazing woman I've ever been with, Lolly Rogers. If we weren't out here on a public walkway, I'd stay like this all night. I may be a middle-aged old geezer, but I feel like a horny teenager around you."

In answer, she kissed him softly. "Me too."

"At least my love handles gave your amazing legs a little cushioning. You okay?"

"Perfect, but I agree...public walkway and all, we might want to keep going."

Suddenly, they heard voices approaching from the south. Laughing, he set her down, and she grabbed her panties from the ground as he cleaned up, zipping his fly. Two teenage couples appeared from the bend below them before she was fully dressed, so she stepped back in the shadows, straightening her bodice and holding her panties behind her. Jack retrieved his jacket and reached for her hand as they stood aside to let the newcomers pass by.

Five minutes later, as the voices faded in the distance, Lolly slipped her panties on. "Do you think they knew what we were doing?"

"Absolutely."

"How embarrassing."

"For them, not us. Besides, kids think no one over thirty has sex, so they probably thought we were birdwatching."

Lolly laughed. "In the dark?"

"Best time for it," he said, laughing as his arm circled her shoulders. He bent to kiss her temple. "Come on, let's get you home."

At her door, he kissed her gently.

"Wish you could stay," she said, running fingers through his hair.

"Me too, but my daughter would be shocked." He kissed her forehead, then her lips.

"Well, good night, then. I had a really good time."

"Me too."

He released her and headed for the car.

"Jack?"

"Yup."

"I love your love handles."

He chuckled. "Well, that's a start. Night, baby."

CHAPTER 34

Lyddie set down her plate and turned to him. "Hey, Dad, this has been a great week. Can I come back again while you're still here?" They were eating breakfast on the back porch. Jack had made omelets, and they had a basket of warm Café muffins and breads with fresh jams, jellies, and farm butter to slather on them.

"My waistline might not survive all this extravagant eating, but of course. Love to have you anytime. Your brother too, if he can spring free."

"Were you serious about the condo idea? I mean, buying something here for you?"

He shrugged. "Still figuring things out. I've grown attached to Barnum's Ledge. It's a beautiful spot. Don't want to sound too corny, but it touches a part of my soul when I look out from that old dilapidated front porch."

"It is very cool, but wouldn't you miss Boston?"

"Not especially. Besides, I can always use the Compass condo or stay in a hotel if I need to be there now and then. As it is, I'm traveling so much for projects that I hardly spend much time at home."

"Well, I vote for finding a place here. Wolfie says he doesn't miss the city at all."

"Oh, he does, does he? Your affinity for this place wouldn't have anything to do with a certain handsome vintner, would it?"

"Yes and no. I've had a really good time with him, that's for sure. But I'd have loved to go riding. Next time, I want to bring my bike and go on the Loop Trail. There's a bunch of other things we didn't get to this trip."

"Anytime, punky."

After saying their goodbyes, Jack hopped in his car and followed Lyddie out to the main road, waving as the cars headed in separate directions, Jack to Morgan's Fire and Lyddie to the Bayport Pike. Even though both were adults now, he still hated saying goodbye to his kids. A feeling of loss always hit him when they parted, not unlike when the family had broken up ten years earlier. He and Cynthia might have been incompatible, but he'd loved their family unit and still mourned its demise. Nothing and no one had quite taken its place.

"I'm so glad to see you, Jen," Lolly said as they strolled back from Saturday-morning breakfast at Netherfield. Sandy had just picked up Maisie, and she was spending Saturday and Sunday nights with Pam and him.

"Me too," Jen said, leaning into her friend. "It's kinda good that Mom's busy with that affair tonight, or her nose would be out of joint if I wasn't spending the day with her."

Since the day Mavis and Duncan LaSalle took Jerry and Jen in after their parents' deaths, both siblings had called her Mom. Usually formal and snobby, Mavis had insisted. The Honeywells had perished in a light plane accident and left their fifteen- and seventeen-year-old daughter and son completely alone, with no other family members to oversee their teenage years. Their dear friends, Mavis and Duncan, had long ago agreed to be the children's guardians and embraced these new roles with warmth and love. Lolly and Jen were the same age, Jerry the same age as their oldest, Duncan

Junior. Jerry and Duncan had gone off to boarding school while the girls stayed in New York City and attended Stuyvesant High School together.

"Mavis's nose is always out of joint about something, but yes, the arrival of Hollywood elite this afternoon will keep her mercifully busy. How's Dad anyway? Weren't you just in the city?"

"You know Dad. Busy, bossy, a new young thing on his arm. This one's younger than we are—Melba. She's a makeup artist for one of the shows." A successful Broadway producer, Duncan LaSalle changed girlfriends with the seasons, and they grew younger each year.

"Yuck."

"I think he still loves Mom. Always has, always will."

Lolly rolled her eyes. "Along with a bevy of young things on the side."

Jen draped her arm over her sister's shoulders. "So enough about the oldsters. How are you? Tell me everything."

"I'll fill you in, if you do the same. I can't believe you're dating Rip Lassitor!"

"I'm not! I'm trying to avoid him at all costs, but it's not easy."

"Oh?" Lolly asked, her tone teasing.

"He's my boss, as I told you. He's also still the most gorgeous, amazing man I've ever seen. I admit it takes a lot of self-restraint to keep from throwing myself at him. What about your guy, 'cause I know there's a guy, right?"

Lolly smiled, her expression dreamy. "There is, kind of. My guy has love handles, and neither of us are spring chickens, but he's pretty amazing."

"Will I meet him?"

"Maybe not this weekend. He's really busy. His daughter's been visiting, and he's in the city tonight."

"He's from New York?"

"Boston."

"Too bad. I'd love to meet him."

"This is a girls' weekend, and neither Jack Faulkner nor Rip

Lassitor are invited! Let's get our suits on and drive down to Moonstone. It's a perfect beach day."

SUNDAY MORNING, JACK PACKED THE REST OF HIS BELONGINGS AND LEFT a large tip for the cleaning staff. Compass's condo on the harbor was beautiful, furnished in muted, tasteful tones, state-of-the-art appliances, and the most comfortable beds in the world, but it wasn't home. The cottage in Horseshoe Crab Cove already seemed more like home than the space where he'd lived the past four months.

CHAPTER 35

Y*up, this feels like home,* Jack thought as he hung his clothes in the closet Sunday afternoon. He still had some things in storage. He'd given most of the furniture in the condo to Marsha and only had Jay's crew store a few family pieces. Mavis had assured him that the cottage was his as long as he wanted it, with a request that, should he still be here in the fall, he would agree to vacate one weekend for some "very special clients." She'd assured him that he would have her best suite at Netherfield for that weekend.

He whistled as he stowed food and clothes, planning the week ahead. They were closing on Barnum's Ledge Wednesday, but the sellers had allowed them to begin demolition. Pete and his crew had already gutted most of the second and third floors and were set to begin on the main floor Monday. It was a risk, but with the kind of money Compass had put down, there was little chance the sellers would pull out without substantial penalties. After a few calls to Pete and Jay, he grabbed a beer and one of the mysteries he'd gotten from Merlin's Closet and headed out to the back porch.

Exhaustion soon took over, and he was awakened by a knock at the front door and a voice calling to him. "Jack, honey! Are you here?" *Marsha.* From the nearness of her voice, it sounded like she was now inside. *Who the hell gave her this address?* he thought as he stood and went in.

It had been sad to say goodbye to Jen. After she departed, Lolly had done a couple of laundry loads, cleaned and vacuumed, then taken a pot of tea and the Sunday papers to the small study off the living room. *How wonderful it has been to have the company of a dear woman friend and sister,* she thought as she settled into the old overstuffed armchair and sipped her tea, the scent and taste of bergamot always soothing. Mavis imported a special blend of Earl Grey tea from England for the Inn and always gave her several boxes when each shipment arrived.

Close as she was to Lucy, her partner and dear friend was married with a very different life than her own. Jen understood the loneliness that crept between the cracks of everyday living, even with her mother nearby and Maisie. Since her ex's marriage, she often found herself sad and empty when Maisie was with him and Pam. She liked Pam Morgan, and was happy for Sandy that he'd found someone like her, but that didn't eradicate the desolate feelings that overcame her when Maisie was with them.

Finally, papers scattered around the floor, teapot empty, she stood up. *Enough wallowing, girl! It's a beautiful night for a beach walk!*

"What are you doing here, Marsha?"

"Is that any way to greet me?"

This can't be happening. He willed himself to be calm and reasonable. Having her standing in his kitchen felt like an invasion. "Look, Marsha, I made things really clear last time we spoke. We are done. The condo's yours, I've visited Poppy, I'm done."

"I have MS."

"What?" He studied her more closely and noticed she looked a little paler than usual and a bit gaunt without the gobs of makeup she usually applied. A ritual he remembered well; her makeup routine took hours. He sure didn't miss the towels and washcloths permanently stained brown and beige from her concealer.

Her jeans and persimmon-colored cotton sweater hung limp on her emaciated frame. *Not unlike Poppy*, he thought as he watched her grab hold of the counter with trembling hands.

"Can we sit?"

"Of course." He gestured toward the living room instead of inviting her to the back porch.

"Might I have a glass of water?" she asked, settling on one of the room's chintz-covered love seats.

He nodded and turned away to grab glasses from the cupboard.

"This is a cute place. However did you find it?"

I could ask you the same question, he thought, handing her the water and taking a seat opposite her. Ignoring her question, he asked, "So what's up?"

"I've been feeling shitty for a while now, and I finally saw the doctor a few weeks ago. They ran some tests, and I'm in the early stages of multiple sclerosis."

"I'm sorry to hear that. Have they developed a plan for you? Treatment-wise, I mean."

She shrugged. "Rest, a bunch of meds, physical therapy, whatever."

"People seem to do okay with MS in a lot of cases."

"And some don't."

"Why are you here? Wouldn't the phone have been easier, especially if you're supposed to be resting?" he asked, his voice weary.

"Phone? That's a little harsh, don't you think? After all we've been through? Besides, we've got to talk about who's going to raise the baby."

"Whoa, stop right there. As Poppy's parents, that's between you and Chuck."

"Poppy hates her father. She won't have anything to do with him."

"He can at least lend some financial support. Set up a trust?" *In too deep, Jack, back away.*

"That's the kind of thinking we need. If you and I put our heads together, I'm sure we can devise a plan."

He swallowed, choosing his words carefully. "We are not together, so there'll be no putting our heads together. Our relationship ended because of your infidelities. Plural. Hurtful, nasty betrayals. I am really sorry about your illness and Poppy's difficulties, but I cannot be in the middle of this," he said, gesturing back and forth between them. "Not anymore. I don't love you, Marsha. In fact, if I'm being truthful, I don't even like you, which is why I gave you the condo, to get you out of my life."

She covered her face with her hands, pretending to cry. He wasn't fooled. The Marsha he'd lived with for almost two years never cried.

He stood, gesturing toward the door. "Let me walk you out so you can get on your way home before dark."

"Hey!" called a voice from the backyard. "Jack, are you there?" *Lolly, terrific. Could this get any worse?*

As she emerged from the woods to the adjacent cottage's backyard, she saw the lights on. *Jack's home! Maybe this is a time for me to be spontaneous?* she thought as she veered from the beach path and approached his back door. "Jack, are you in there?" she called as she opened the screen door and stepped onto the porch.

Instantly, he appeared at the kitchen door. "Hey, hi!" he called, an odd expression on his face.

Before either of them could say another word, Marsha called from inside the house, "Hey, babe, who's that?" A thin brunette popped her head around the door, hand on Jack's shoulder. Her face sepulchral and shiny, her head, like a bobblehead doll, wobbled atop her swizzle-stick body. Like talons, bright red fingernails gripped Jack's shoulders.

Lolly's stomach lurched, and she stepped back, raising her arms as if protecting herself. "Oh...sorry, I didn't realize you had company."

"Well, he does," Marsha purred, fake tears forgotten. "I'm Marsha, his girlfriend. And you are?"

Lolly took another step backward. "So sorry for interrupting. Headed for a beach walk and thought I'd take a chance."

"Wait, Loll," he said, shrugging out of Marsha's grasp as he crossed the porch.

Lolly turned and broke into a run, trying to reach the beach path before he caught her. "Please, Lolly. It's not what you think."

She paused, facing him. "No problem. You have company. I should have called."

"No, you shouldn't have. What I mean is you can stop by anytime."

"Not now, apparently," she said, angry tears rimming her eyes as she glimpsed a woman in the shadows of the porch.

He took hold of her arms, eyes pleading. "She just showed up to tell me she's sick. I have no idea how she even knew where to find me."

She wriggled out of his grasp. "Well, you'd better get back to her, then."

"Listen to me. She means nothing to me."

"I've got to go," she said, turning away.

"I'll call you," he yelled after her.

She gave no response as she plunged into the woods, tears blurring her vision as she hurried forward. *Stupid, stupid, stupid,* she thought as the beach came into view. Afraid he might eventually follow or come to her cottage, she decided to head to Netherfield and stay the night.

One look at her and Mavis opened her arms. "Okay, sweetie, I'm here."

"My cell's at home, Mom. I want Maisie to be able to get me."

"No worries. You come in, and I'll call Sandy. Let Mama take care of you tonight."

~

JACK TURNED AND STALKED TO THE HOUSE. "MARSHA, TIME FOR YOU TO head out. I've got things to do."

"What? Go run after your bimbo? I see you're going for full-figured these days. What an ass on that one."

All the anger of the past year boiled up, and before he could stop himself, he said, "Marsha, shut the hell up. Grab your purse and get out of my house. Now!"

"You mean your rental property, don't you?" she snapped, eyes blazing. "Can I use the little ladies' before I leave?"

Little ladies'. He hated that expression. Not trusting himself to speak, he nodded his head, indicating the bathroom.

When she emerged several minutes later, she'd applied fresh lipstick and swept her hair back. "No chance of taking this little lady to dinner, is there?"

What do you think? "I've got a lot to do. Let's go." He opened the front door for her, following her out to her dark Burgundy convertible.

"I'll be in touch," she said as he opened her door and she slipped in.

"I'd rather you weren't. I wish you good luck, I really do, but I can't do this anymore. If you get in a jam and want to be in touch, do it through Jay."

"That vulture. Dream on."

"Well, suit yourself, but I'm going to ask him to handle any and all future communications between us."

"Fuck you, Jack!" she said. Her tires spun on the driveway as she backed up and peeled off.

That's about right, he thought, having lost count of how many times this scene had played out over the last year and a half. Jay had urged him to get a restraining order. *Time to make that call, buddy*, he thought.

CHAPTER 36

The days went by, and Jack's calls to Lolly went straight to voicemail. He left numerous texts and voice messages, all of which went unanswered. He heard nothing more from Marsha. Jay had put the restraining order in place and had also had someone from his office stop by the condo. He had the door slammed in his face, but the message had been delivered. Jack called Farrell Park once each week and chatted briefly with Liza Romano, asking that she keep his calls to herself.

Barnum's Ledge was well underway, demolition almost complete. The architects were still tweaking plans for the renovations, especially with the additions Jack had requested. When he had spare time, Jack headed out to Morgan's Fire to check on the restaurant's progress. Sam and his team of architects had completed the plans, and the groundbreaking took place on a sunny afternoon to great fanfare. A small group of family and townspeople attended, including Rosa and Cesar Rodriguez and several of Sandy's brothers and sisters. Lolly, Mavis, and Maisie also came, as did Jack. When he tried to speak to Lolly, she waved him away, requesting that he leave her alone.

Richard had witnessed the tortured interaction. As they walked back to the farm after the groundbreaking, he found Jack. "Hey, buddy, thanks so much for coming. The kids tell me your help's been invaluable."

"My pleasure," Jack said, distracted by the group walking ahead of them, which included Lolly, Lucy, and Richard's daughters, Maisie skipping along beside them with Ava's kids.

"She'll come around, you'll see. I love my wife's business partner, but she's as stubborn and pigheaded a woman as I've ever met, and that's saying something with four strong-willed daughters."

Jack shook his head, thinking how pretty Lolly looked today in ass-hugging jeans and a sleeveless jersey, a sweater draped around her shoulders, her hair pulled back in a loose ponytail. "You may be right, but not today."

"Give it time."

"That's my intention."

"You're welcome to stay for supper."

"Thanks, but Lyddie's coming in for the weekend."

"You should go grab her and come right back. I know someone here who'd love to see her."

Jack chuckled. "Hence the reason for her visit. Thanks for the invite, but she's requested that we eat at Blue Water so she can have 'Dad night,' because she and your son have the rest of the weekend planned, and I'm pretty sure that none of their activities include dear old Dad."

Richard clapped him on the shoulder. "Young love, ain't it grand?"

Glad someone's in love, Jack mused as he headed for his car.

Weeks went by as Barnum's Ledge progressed. Roland had been down a few times to check on progress and was very impressed. Jack had seen Lolly from a distance in town and as she and Maisie walked by on their way to the beach, but had decided to leave her alone and concentrate on something over which he had control.

Miserable and lonely, Lolly threw herself into work. They hired a local carpenter to build shelving in their office as well as in their section of the Morgan's Fire barn. Lynn Casey was now working two days a week for them. They had participated in several fairs and were hard at work on their fall catalog. When Lucy suggested they take a vacation. Lolly's reply had been, "You do what you want, but I need to work right now to hold on to sanity." Sandy and Pam had Maisie for two weeks, during one of which they were going camping in Maine, so she really needed to keep busy. She took two trips, one to New York City to visit her dad, the other to stay with Jen for a weekend. Time with her dad meant a different play every night and sometimes a matinee too. Time with Jen had been more relaxed, with time for tubing down the local river and kayaking too.

When she returned, Maisie was still away. She'd done a lot of thinking while at Jen's and decided she was ready. *Time to clear the air and move on*, she thought, *since who knows how long he'll be here working on both projects.*

She grabbed her phone and punched in his number. He answered on the first ring. "Hey."

"Hi."

"Great to hear your voice."

"Yours too. Listen, Jack, can we talk? If you're going to be in the village for a while, I think we need to clear the air and be direct... about where we stand."

"Of course. This isn't a great time 'cause my boss is here today. How about we meet up tomorrow? You free?"

"Maisie's away, so I'm pretty much always free." *The loser that I am!*

"How about we meet here at the Ledge tomorrow? Maybe around six? I'll grab a bottle of wine, and we can sit on the spanking new deck. Love to show you around."

"Great, see you then," she said, clicking off and sighing. His voice was like a smooth tonic, soothing to her frayed emotions.

CHAPTER 37

Still at loose ends and lonely, Lolly decided to walk to town for breakfast. The warmth of the Café and her fellow villagers never failed to buoy her spirits. No matter when you visited the always-crowded restaurant, you were sure to find someone you knew and an invitation to join them if you chose to do so. As she scanned the room, Lolly spied Lucy's sister Harriet and waved. Harriet's companion was back to her, but she recognized the curly mop of hair as belonging to Karen Miller. Harriet gestured for her to join them, and Lolly put up one finger and mouthed, *Be right over.*

Five minutes later, bagel and coffee in hand, she greeted the two women. "Are you sure this is okay? I'm not interrupting your gal time?"

"You're a gal, aren't you?" Karen said, patting the chair next to her. Harriet and Karen had been the "little kids" in high school. Like everyone in the village, they felt like family, all of them Darn Yarner offspring.

"Haven't seen you around much this summer," Lolly said, sitting next to the petite rancher with lapis-blue eyes and a rosy face sprayed with freckles. "How're you doing? Hip okay?" Karen had been seriously injured in a farm accident and had undergone a hip replacement and many months of painful therapy.

"Doin' great. Not jogging with my fiancé yet, but the doc says it's possible. At least I can ride."

"Carefully," Harriet said, winking at Lolly. Though her smile was so like her older sister's, Harriet's chestnut hair was longer and darker than Lucy's, and her eyes were an intense jade green.

"Believe me, I've seen her on the Loop. Always the daredevil." Lolly referred to the eighteen-mile Loop Trail that circled the peninsula and the village, passing through Mavis's property, then on to Land's End, Karen's family's farm.

"Haven't seen your little cutie at the stables lately," Karen said. "Has she given up riding?"

Lolly wrinkled her nose. "Please don't be mad, but Weezie Morgan begged me to put her in the pony camps at Morgan's Fire this summer."

"No worries. We don't run the camps anymore and have scaled way back on lessons except for our regulars. Even your mom hasn't sent anyone recently." Mavis had an agreement with Land's End Stables, and her guests sometimes rode from there.

"Thanks for understanding. She's does love riding and loves being with all the kids. She's one of the youngest, and they all take care of her. Your future sister-in-law's great with kids too." Karen was engaged to the eldest Morgan, Rich.

Karen nodded. "Sure is."

"Where is your handsome fiancé today and, for that matter, your gorgeous husband?" she asked, turning to Harriet.

"Kyle's out at Land's End with a mare about to give birth," Harriet replied.

"And Rich is meeting with his dad and the team out at Field and Fire. As you know, Pam and Sandy are away, but they corralled Jack to help them with something today, who knows what."

"So they've got a name for the restaurant?" Lolly asked, suddenly feeling out of touch.

Karen nodded. "Tentative. They've gotta get going with PR and branding. Rich says they're committed to making the final decision by next week."

"Field and Fire. I like it," Lolly said.

"Me too," Karen said. "So what's new with you? You still seeing Jack? He and Rich have gotten pretty friendly, which is great because Rich doesn't have a lot of buddies in town. We're trying to convince him to stay around."

Lolly gulped. "We... I haven't seen much of him for a few weeks now."

"He's a great guy," Harriet said, sipping her tea, kind eyes regarding her older sister's friend.

"Yes, he is. It's complicated."

"Isn't every relationship?" Karen waved her toast. "Look at Rich and me. Or even you guys." She gestured toward Harriet.

Lolly smiled at her partner's sister. She'd heard enough from Lucy about their earlier life, then Harriet's traumatic college relationship to know that the beautiful woman sitting across from them had gone through hell and back. "Well, we're getting together tonight to clear the air, so stay tuned. If nothing else, I'm determined that we'll end up friends."

"That's the spirit!" Karen said, slapping the table.

As she walked home, Lolly wondered if it had been a mistake to confide about her get-together with Jack to Karen especially. *How fast will it get from one end of Horseshoe Crab Cove to the other?* she mused, waving to a group of gardeners as she passed Laura's Community Garden, the brainchild of her ex's wife, Pam. The garden was a wonderful space, created and enjoyed by the entire town on land originally belonging to Mavis LaSalle. They were talking about more acreage next year as garden plots were in high demand.

CHAPTER 38

After his return from Morgan's Fire, Jack showered and changed, grabbing a basket from the kitchen into which he put wineglasses, cheese and crackers, and a nice bottle of Pinot Noir. He smiled as he assembled the mini picnic. He had high hopes for the evening. He'd missed Lolly more than he'd ever missed any woman. That he was crazy in love with her, he was certain. *Now how to convince her that I'm worth another chance?*

A warm night, the sky was clear and blanketed with stars as he parked and carried the basket to the porch. After straightening up the table and chairs, he sat, waiting. This was a huge step for him, especially after Marsha and the divorce, but he was surer than he'd ever been about anyone or anything. He didn't have to wait long before her Volvo turned into the drive. Jack stood and walked down to greet her, marveling as he always did at her earthy beauty. Even in jeans and a casual gray sweater, she looked like a goddess.

"Hey," he called, as she waved.

Suddenly shy, Lolly said, "Hi," holding up the bottle she'd brought. "I see you already have wine, but I wasn't sure."

He smiled, glad to see her. "The night is young." They hugged briefly, his lips brushing her cheek. "I've missed you, babe," he whispered, voice husky.

Lolly stepped back, flustered, her body on fire. He was talking, but all she could think about was flinging herself at him, begging him to drag her into the nearest dark corner. "I'm sorry, what did you say?"

Jack grinned. "I asked if you'd like wine."

"Love it." She followed him to the porch and stood as he uncorked the bottle and poured.

"You've made incredible progress out here."

"My guys are the best. Want a tour?"

She nodded as he handed her the glass, fingers brushing her hand and sending shivers up her arm. "That'd be great."

"Okay, welcome to Barnum's Ledge." He swung open the original carved mahogany front doors, now fully restored, and they stepped into the lobby and came face-to-face with the grand sweeping staircase. On either side open, glass-walled parlors were in various states of refurbishing.

Lolly stared openmouthed. "Is this the way it was?"

"Staircase is original and footprint's the same, but we took down the parlor walls here and here to open things up. This hall's so wide, we're planning to have reception right here," he said, waving toward an alcove on the west side of the hall. He smiled. "Pretty cool, isn't it?"

"It's incredible!" *How could the man have grown more handsome and sexy in just four weeks? Or had I just forgotten what I was missing?* "You must be so pleased."

He shrugged. "It's a job, but it's been satisfying so far, can't deny that. Come on. The upstairs rooms are still works in progress, but it's a trip to climb this staircase. He held out his hand, and she took it, his warmth suffusing her from head to toe.

As they peeked into each room, Jack flipped a wall switch, illuminating single bulbs dangling from each ceiling. "All this is temporary work lighting. The original fixtures are either down for repair or we've ordered new ones. One of our designers just ordered all the paint and wallpaper. The bathrooms are gutted and waiting for tiles and fixtures. Third floor's storage, but I want to show you something." He led her to the end of the hall and opened a narrow door opening onto a narrow, winding staircase illuminated by a single dangling lightbulb. "I've always been a sucker for back staircases. This is one of my favorite spaces in the inn."

As they descended, she brushed against his back, several times falling against him. "I hope this isn't for guests."

At the bottom, he turned to her, hand on the small of her back. "Only really special ones," he whispered.

"Jack... I don't know...I—"

"Here we are!" he said, swinging open a door that brought them into the cavernous state-of-the-art kitchen. Miles of countertop ringed the room with its multiple refrigerators, freezers, ovens, dishwashers, and an enormous twenty-burner Vulcan stove. A central island ran the length of the room, gleaming stainless steel and copper pots hanging above it. The space's most striking feature, however, were the columns that stood throughout, their ridged surfaces cresting into palm trees at the ceiling. The ceiling lights hung from enormous fans, their blades like giant dragonfly wings.

"Wow!" she said, gazing upward. "It's beautiful."

"Should be. Most expensive room in the house."

"It's so unusual. Were the palm trees here? They're very cool, but it seems an odd choice for this location."

"The room's modeled after Brighton Palace. Don't ask me why, but the previous owner did it in the forties, and I think it's cool, so we kept it. It was a bitch to restore those palms, excuse my language."

"I've never been there. To Brighton, I mean."

"Me neither, but I'd love to take you someday."

She smiled, the soft warm smile he liked to think was his alone. From his observations, the public Lolly rarely let down her guard to smile like that. "Come on," he said, grabbing her hand again. "There's more out back."

He led her through a hallway of pantries, their shelves newly painted, glass fronts replaced and repaired, before they stepped out the inn's back door. There were a number of outbuildings on the property, but the one that immediately caught her eye was new. Where a small cabana had once been, a two-story shingled cottage sat on the cliffs, a wide porch circling it on three sides. It was framed and sided, but the interior appeared to be unfinished.

"What a great addition," she said. "This'll be booked three years in advance once people see it."

Grinning, he squeezed her hand. "Not for rent."

"Why not?"

"Because it's mine."

Incredulous, she stared at him. "Excuse me? Yours? You're staying... You're not going back to the city?"

His blue eyes held hers as he drew her closer. "You seem pretty attached to Horseshoe Crab Cove."

"That's me... I mean I am, and Maisie's dad is... Well, it would be tricky." They were still standing on the inn's back stoop, and she broke away and descended the stairs to the lawn. "Wait a minute... I came here to say...I wanted to tell you."

"Come on," he said. "Don't get tongue-tied on me, babe. Plenty of time to talk."

Incredulous, she followed him into the cottage. The views were spectacular, and the open floor plan took full advantage of the location. "Like it?" he asked as they stood in the bare bones of what would be the kitchen.

"It's amazing, but I don't understand," she said, gazing up at him.

Jack took her wineglass and placed it and his own on a nearby stool. "Course you don't, because I haven't asked you a very important question."

"Oh?"

Before she knew what was happening, he knelt on one knee in a pile of sawdust. He then reached up and took both her hands. "Lolly Rogers, I know we've only known each other a short time, but I am crazy in love with you. I cannot imagine living anywhere where I can't see you every day. The past four weeks have been torture, but this place has kept me going."

"Jack, you're getting filthy. What are you doing down there?"

"I'm asking you to marry me. I know you'll think I'm crazy, and I fully expect you to say no, but I'm asking now and will give you all the time you need because there will never be anyone else for me." He reached into his jacket and pulled out a small box, opening it to reveal a beautiful diamond in a delicate antique setting.

She gasped. "Oh, Jack!"

"This isn't a bribe. It's a gift to ask you to think about my proposal. Give it time, and when and if you're ready, we can—" He looked up aghast to see tears streaming down her cheeks. "Oh, geez, I've done it now. Lolly, I'm so sorry... This is too soon. I've freaked you out, and pretty soon you're going to run out of here and—"

"Yes."

"Yes, you're gonna run?"

"No...yes, I will marry you! If you're crazy enough to ask me, yes, yes, yes!" she cried, jumping into his arms as they both fell over, rolling in sawdust.

"Babe, much as I'd love to ravish you this second, an old geezer like me has some limitations. Come on," he said, rolling them over and helping her up. He grabbed a whisk broom and brushed down her, then himself. "That's better. Now for the best part. You haven't seen the master bedroom."

Hands over her eyes, he led her down a hallway, nudging a door open and guiding her in. She could hear the flick of a light switch before he removed his hands to reveal a three-foot-high air mattress covered with a white quilt that was strewn with rose petals. Lolly leaned her head back, nuzzling his neck. "It's perfect."

"And so are you," he whispered, hands moving up to cradle her breasts. "I've missed you, baby."

She could feel him growing hard against her and she began a rhythmic rubbing up and down, the feel of him like liquid fire. "You have no idea how much I've missed you too, Jack. I'm literally burning up with wanting you."

"Well, we can't have that now, can we?" he growled. He slipped her sweater over her head, as she reached around to unhook her bra and fling it to the floor. His hands were everywhere, lips trailing down the back of her neck, driving her blind with desire. Slowly, he unbuttoned her jeans as she simultaneously reached around to unzip him, releasing his throbbing cock, caressing and stroking the way she knew he loved.

With one strong move, he swept her into his arms. "That's all I can stand, baby. I spent a lot of time finding that comfy air mattress, and that's where I'm taking you." He laid her down and spread her legs, his fingers probing gently as he slipped a condom on and moved over her.

"No, my love," she said, gazing into his eyes as he entered her. "You're taking me to the moon, and I don't ever want to come back!"

Lolly's legs twined around him, pulling him deeper as she matched him thrust for thrust. "Yes, yes, yes," she cried as they moved in tandem to a roaring climax that left them both drenched in sweat, completely satiated as they collapsed in each other's arms.

He pulled back slightly, kissing her forehead, cheeks, nose, then lips. "Guess it's a good thing I bought a top-of-the-line model. Otherwise, we'd have popped this sucker for sure."

She nuzzled his neck. "You're so crude, aren't you?"

"And proud of it."

"I love you," she said, gazing into his beautiful eyes, lost in their blue depths.

"Back at you, babe, more than I could ever tell you."

She smiled, fingers caressing his jaw. "I don't know, you've been doing a pretty good job expressing yourself tonight. I was afraid I might never get a word in edgewise."

"And I was scared shitless that if I stopped talking, you'd have time to say no."

"Never. Now, will I ever get a chance to try on that beautiful ring?"

"Thought you'd never ask." He reached down to retrieve his pants from the floor and opened the box to reveal the ring, a lovely diamond in an antique setting surrounded by tiny sapphires.

As he slipped it onto her finger, Lolly smiled, gazing up at him. "I'm really happy right now."

"Me too, sweetheart. I'm going to try to make every day this happy for you for the rest of our lives."

"That's very ambitious, don't you think?" she asked, smiling as she nibbled playfully on his shoulder.

"Not when you're motivated like I am."

She felt him stir inside her, growing and filling her. "Speaking of motivated," she said, kissing him as they began their dance again, this time slowly, languidly, lovingly. They moved to an intense, deeply felt climax that left them warm and peaceful.

Much later, they emerged from the cottage arm in arm. "I'm starving," she said, "And I don't think your cheese and crackers will satisfy me."

"Hmm," he said, checking his watch. "Just after nine. The Grille serves till ten, right?"

"It does, but I'm not sure we're fit to be seen in public. Everyone'll know exactly what we've been doing."

Jack kissed her temple, pulling her close. "Good, I want them to know. Then, right after, we can announce our engagement!"

She turned to face him, standing on tiptoes, her lips finding his for a quick kiss. "While I'd like nothing more than to shout the news from every rooftop in town, I want to wait and tell Maisie first. Is that okay? She's been kind of confused the last few weeks, missing you and not understanding where you were and why we weren't seeing you."

"I've missed her too. Of course it's okay," he said, his eyes full of love as he pulled her closer. "Our number one flower girl should definitely be the first to know."

～

Read on for sample chapters of *Emma's Dream*, book one of the Morgan's Run series.

EMMA'S DREAM

Chapter One

"This is a huge mistake," Ben Morgan muttered, his chest tightening as he steered the Range Rover over the Arizona mountain pass. "Maybe the biggest one I've made in five years."

Then he remembered it wasn't his decision. Doctor's orders propelled him eastward, away from his gorgeous new home in Santa Barbara and a rapidly expanding business, which needed his attention twenty-four seven. The partners, his college roommates and dear friends, had assured him they could manage without him for a while, but the guilt was eating at him already. His stomach growled, but there was no place to stop in the desert that surrounded him. He would have to eat in town.

As the jeep climbed the Saguaro Canyon Pass, he thought back to the previous Thursday. On the Coast Highway, headed home for a swim in the ocean after a long day at work, he was still reeling from his last encounter with Miranda, his girlfriend of two years. Their official split had been several months earlier, when he moved out of their condo and into his new home, but unfinished business, mostly financial, had necessitated one more meeting, over lunch. The parting hadn't been pleasant, but they still needed to work together.

Miranda's law firm handled all his company's legal work, and the partners wanted to keep her on.

As he exited the restaurant, the pain started. Chalking it up to indigestion, he'd hopped in the car and endeavored to ignore it. Halfway home, the pain now excruciating, he almost blacked out but was able to pull over and call 911. He told the operator he was having a heart attack.

Several hours and a battery of tests later, the cardiologist smiled as she leaned over his gurney. "Fascinating diagnosis, Mr. Morgan, but totally incorrect. You've had a panic attack. I'm not sure what's going on in your life right now, but whatever it is, you'd better see that it stops now."

"So, I'm crazy? Is that what you're saying?"

"No, what I'm saying is that something's going on that's triggering your physical symptoms. Are you under a lot of stress? Did anything unusual happen today?"

"Just work and the end of a romantic relationship."

She shook her head, regarding him as one might a two-year-old. "Two huge stressors. Do you have a cardiologist?"

"Why should I? I'm thirty-one, for Christ's sake."

"Right, okay. Well then, let's pretend I'm your cardiologist. As your doctor, I am ordering you to take at least three to four months off work to decompress."

"Three to four months! Now you're the crazy one. I have a business to run and—"

"Which you won't be running for long if the stress and anxiety cause a massive heart attack. Either take time now to decompress, reevaluate, and learn ways to live your life differently, or we'll be spending a lot more time together. Do I make myself clear?"

Now, six days later, he was headed to his family's ranch in Arizona, Morgan's Run, and his enforced R & R. He laughed, wondering if returning home might actually increase his stress rather than the opposite. The Rover crested the peak, and he began his descent into the verdant valley that stretched out north and south as far as the eye could see. An orographic effect created this green, moist valley, surrounded by desert over the mountains to the east and west. In the gorgeous valley, a largely undiscovered town existed, an oasis for its roughly three thousand year-round residents and an equal number of snowbirds, tourists, and wealthy vacationers who found their way through the passes at various points in the year.

As Ben Junior made his way into town, he passed familiar sights, largely unchanged. Nothing changed much in Saguaro. The Town Garage had a fresh coat of white paint. "Whoop-de-doo," he said aloud, making a mental note to drop the Rover off for servicing soon.

As he turned right on Main and headed toward Gracie's Diner, a horn blared and the clunker in front of him screeched to a stop. Ben braked, but not in time to stop the Rover before it tapped the rear of the clunker. Ben swore under his breath and backed up, pulling over to park at the curb. As he did, the clunker's driver leaped from her car, screaming and waving her arms. He shook his head. Foolish woman had left her heap in the middle of the street. Tall and slender, she wore Jackie O. sunglasses, a baseball cap pulled low on her forehead, a faded cotton shirt over blue jeans, and cowboy boots, the uniform for nearly every female rancher in the valley.

"Geez, Toto," he muttered, patting the Rover's seat. "We're not in Kansas anymore."

As she approached the Rover, Ben noticed her jeans hugged every curve, full breasts not quite obscured by the baggy shirt. He couldn't see her face, but he had to admit the rest of the package was intriguing and also vaguely familiar. He approached as she bent to survey the clunker's bumper.

"What's the matter with you?" she screamed, walking in circles, arms still flailing. "Oh my God, oh my God, what am I going to do?"

Ben stared at her back, astounded at what was clearly a huge overreaction. Her car was fine, hardly a scratch on it, although it would be hard to tell with all the other dings. Then, just as quickly as it started, the fire went out and she flopped down to sit on the curb, head between her legs, sobbing.

"Hey, hey, it's not that bad, is it? We hardly touched each other. No harm done." He sat beside her, wondering whether he should pat her on the shoulder. Immediately, she quieted and looked up at him.

"Oh my God. This just gets better and better. It figures."

Ben Morgan, the one person she expected never to see again, was sitting beside her. Could things get any worse? She leaned forward, hiding her face, wondering whether he'd go away if she sat there long enough.

"Maggie? Is that little Maggie Williams? After five years, I'm in town less than a minute, and the first person I bump into is you."

Maggie groaned and buried her head deeper in her arms, praying this was all a bad dream. If she hadn't had to make a quick run to the bank, she'd be at work in the cool, dark stables. "Please just go. I'm fine."

She could feel his heat, his nearness rattling her to her core. A part of her longed to lean against him and draw comfort and strength from his warmth, but the wiser half screamed *danger*. She kept still, hoping he would disappear.

"You don't seem fine. Look, I'm sorry." Ben placed a hand on her shoulder. It sent shivers of warmth all the way to her toes. "And I'm not leaving until I'm sure you're okay."

Oh no, you don't. Maggie stood and shook herself, stepping away from his electric touch. She put on her sunglasses. Another second near him and she feared she might actually swoon. His soft chestnut eyes regarded her with obvious concern. Although he looked tired and thin, Ben Morgan was still drop-dead gorgeous, in faded jeans and sneakers, his broad shoulders straining the seams of a worn Stanford T-shirt.

"I'm fine, really. It's been a crazy day, and you caught me at a bad time. I'm sorry I overreacted."

Ben watched her, wondering why a fender kiss had caused so much distress. "Can I give you a lift somewhere?"

"No, of course not! I mean, thanks, but I'm okay now. No worries about the car. No need to get police involved. Got to get back to work."

"Where's that?"

"Sorry, I'm really late. Good to see you again. Take care."

She hopped into her car and drove away before he could utter another word.

What the hell was that? Ben thought back to his one memorable night with Maggie Williams. They had both left Saguaro shortly after that night, but a part of him always wondered if there was something more to explore with his brother Kyle's beautiful classmate. While he'd pushed thoughts of her and their one night of passionate sex from his mind, as he watched her drive away, Ben realized that he'd spent five years comparing every woman he met to Maggie Williams. His stomach growled, and he shook his head. *Enough, time to eat!* He left the Rover and walked the three blocks to Gracie's.

Chapter Two

Noon rush over, Gracie's was empty except for one booth occupied by a family of four savoring the last spoonfuls of a Gracie Gila Monster. The diner's signature sundae was made with Gracie's secret chocolate sauce, vanilla ice cream, and hot toffee sauce, topped with whipped cream, then sprinkled liberally with crumbled peanut butter cups. Ben was tempted to forgo lunch and go for a Gila, but decided on a portabella burger instead. With a nod to the family, he sidled up and took a stool at the counter.

A young freckle-faced redhead, ponytail wagging, bounced up, flashing him a smile that lit up the room. "Hi, sir. Can I take your order?"

"Hi, yourself. I don't know you. Are you new in town?"

She regarded him quizzically with lots of eyelash batting. "No, but you are. I'd remember you. Been here three years. I'm a student at U of A, but summers I come up to Saguaro instead of goin' home to Yuma. Too hot. My dad works down there. Just passing through?"

Ben gave her the hundred-watt smile that made most women swoon. She was no exception. "You could say that. Name's Ben."

"I'm Stacy. What can I get you, Ben?"

"Iced tea and a portabella burger, lettuce, tomato, and lots of Gracie's burger sauce."

"Comin' right up."

Ben watched her disappear into the kitchen, relieved that he hadn't yet met anyone he knew. He wanted to surprise his parents.

Well—he *had* met someone, he mused, remembering the curvaceous, lush-lipped Maggie Williams. It had been all he could do not to sweep her into his arms and kiss away those tears. Once again, he wondered at the subconscious torch he'd been carrying for her. And what was with her behavior? *Who falls apart and sobs uncontrollably over a bumper tap?*

Half an hour later, as he savored the last bite of his burger, Gracie emerged from the kitchen. "Still a vegetarian, I see. Crime in God's country."

Ben stood as she came around the counter to grab him in a bear hug. At six-four, he had her by a few inches, but Gracie was at least six feet herself, a towering figure in a grease-covered apron and frayed jeans, her wiry black hair streaked with gray, cut short, and sticking out at odd angles.

"How's my desert goddess? Have you missed me? You look younger than when I left."

"Tush." She waved her hand, clearly pleased by the compliment. "Always were the biggest liar from here to Albuquerque. Are you home to stay?"

"No, just a break from the rat race."

"Your folks must be thrilled. Can't believe they won't be angling for you to stay on, what with your dad slowing down and your brothers scattered hither and yon."

"Is Dad okay?"

Gracie gave him a measured look before answering. "Course he is. Strong as an ox, but he's not twenty-five anymore. Could use the help, I'm sure."

"Gracie, this is me. Has something happened to Dad?"

"He's fine, dearie. Had a minor dustup last year, but from your expression, I guess he didn't tell you about it. Not my place. Let him or your mom fill you in."

He stared at her for a moment or two, knowing he wouldn't get another word out of her. "If you could keep my arrival quiet till I see them, I'd be grateful, Gracie."

Ben went for his wallet, suddenly anxious to be home.

Gracie waved her hand. "Not on your life! Put that city money away and git up there and say howdy-do to your folks."

He leaned over and pecked her cheek. "Thanks, Gracie. Great to see you."

"Good to have you home where you belong," she said, gently nudging him toward the door. "Hope it's for good."

Chapter Three

Maggie drove through the main gate of Morgan's Run and pulled into her usual spot behind the stables. She killed the engine and drew out her cell phone. When her father answered, she breathed a sigh of relief.

"How's my angel?" she asked.

"Good as gold," he replied. "What's the matter, sweetie? You sound upset."

"Nothing, just wanted to check in on you and Emma."

"She's napping. Should I phone when she wakes so you can say hello?"

"No, I'll see her in a few hours."

"Mags, what is it? What's happened?"

"Ben Morgan's back."

"Oh? Bump into each other, did you?"

"You could say that. We had a fender bender, right on Main Street."

"You okay?"

"Yes, just embarrassed. When it happened, I freaked out. Made a total fool of myself, crying and wailing over a minor bumper tap. Thank goodness no one else was around."

"Glad you're okay. You gonna tell him about Emma?"

A truck drove up beside her, and Maggie spied Jeb, her assistant.

"Dad, I gotta go. See you tonight."

"Take care, honey."

Maggie waved to her assistant. "Hey, Jeb. You ready to tackle Tabasco?"

She referred to a spirited mustang they were training, the size of a small draft horse. Soon, his rider, a Border Patrol agent, would join them to participate in the final weeks of training. Then horse and rider would return to Nogales as a team, ready to keep watch in the mountains along the border.

"Ready when you are. You okay, boss? You look a little green around the gills."

"Fine, just tired."

"How's my little cutie pie Emma doin'?"

"Full of it, curious, into everything, just like most four-year-olds. She keeps my dad busy."

"How's the therapy going?"

"Not much progress. She's just outgrown her third wheelchair."

"Wow, has it been that long since the accident?"

Maggie nodded. The sadness sometimes overwhelmed her, etching new lines across her brow and haunting her dreams. Afraid to be far from her phone, she watched the clock until it was time to head home. It wasn't that she disliked the work. Maggie loved training horses, assisting with the day-to-day running of Morgan Run's stables, but she worried constantly about Emma. Two years ago, the toddler had just learned to walk when their car had been broadsided by a drunk driver.

Hands on hips, she stared at Jeb, who seemed a million miles away. "Are you coming or not?"

"Sorry, boss!"

He fell in step beside her as they headed for Tabasco's stall.

Chapter Four

Ben eased the Rover through the front gates, turned away from the house, and headed for the lodge. At this time of day, he was pretty certain Ben Sr. would be in the lobby bar greeting guests, offering them a drink and a handshake. Ben Junior parked and hopped out of the Rover, pausing to gaze up at the massive log structure. Newly restored from a much smaller building, the renovated lodge had been designed by his brother Sam, an architect who lived and worked in Flagstaff. Its new wings spread in either direction as if the lodge were a colossal condor ready to take flight.

Ben sprang up the steps and passed through the massive twelve-foot doors that stood open to the afternoon breezes. He scanned the lobby until he caught sight of his dad. At six-foot-six, Ben Morgan was hard to miss. A thick shock of gray hair curled at his collar, and deep blue eyes sparkled with warmth as he chatted with a group of guests.

As Ben approached, the elder Morgan spied him and paused midsentence. "S'cuse me, folks," he said, nodding as he extracted himself. He closed the gap to his son, arms open. "Well, look who's home."

After a hearty bear hug, Ben Sr. patted his progeny. "What're you tryin' to do, give this old man a heart attack?"

"Hey, Dad."

"Has your mother seen you?"

"Not yet. Just got here. Wanted to see you first. See how things are."

"Great, couldn't be better. Especially now that you're home. How long you stayin'?"

"A month or two, maybe more. If it's okay?"

"Okay? You kidding? We'll take you as long as we can get you. Forever would be great."

"Thanks, Dad."

"Better get over to see your ma, or she'll have my hide. I'll finish up the meet-and-greet and be over shortly."

"You look good, Dad," Ben said, and he meant it. His father hadn't aged a bit, his long, lean body in terrific shape, as always.

Remembering Gracie's words, he hoped that whatever had befallen his beloved parent had been resolved.

"Pshaw. Go on, now, git. Be down in a few."

Ben started down the lane to the house, but decided to take the long way around the stables. As he turned the corner, coming round the north side of the barn, there she was, standing beside the clunker, talking on her cell phone. She was bare-headed now, her sunglasses perched atop her head, holding back her long, thick chestnut mane, loose and falling around her shoulders. She was smiling, in animated conversation, a musical laugh punctuating her words. She was gorgeous, the gangly teenager all grown up, transformed into a voluptuous woman. Ben thought about Miranda. Stylish and chic, but oh so skinny, a toothpick compared to this full-bodied, luscious creature. *Totally different species.*

Suddenly, Maggie caught sight of him, and the smile vanished. Her loose, open stance closed up, and she turned away.

"Emma, honey, gotta go. See you soon, sweet pea."

Turning back, Maggie watched Ben step from the Rover and steeled herself for another encounter. The man was magnificent, no doubt about that. To her annoyance, her treacherous body began to tingle from head to toe.

"Mr. Morgan, we meet again."

"What brings you to the ranch?"

"I work here."

"Oh?" Despite her defiant stance, he noticed that her lip trembled. *Don't know how I can change the dynamic between us, but she's sure worth a try.*

"I train horses, run the pony camps and lessons, and help organize most of the pack trips. Harley leads them, of course, and I do the day-to-day stuff." *You're babbling, Maggie Williams. Stop talking!*

"What happened to Princeton?"

"Dropped out."

"Why?"

"Look, it's been a long day. I've got to get going."

"Do you live here? On the ranch?"

"No. Still live in town with my dad."

"How's he doing?"

Ben racked his brain to think of conversation topics that might keep her talking. Gazing into those deep azure eyes, he discovered a warmth and stillness he'd never experienced before. Had it been that way during the one night they'd spent together? He didn't remember those eyes, but he could still feel her soft skin, still smell her scent, a mix of citrus and jasmine.

"He's terrific. Same old, same old."

"Still wrangling and taking care of the valley livestock?"

"He retired a few years ago, but he keeps busy."

"Give him my best."

Gazing into his warm, dark eyes, Maggie felt herself going weak at the knees. And there was that treacherous tingle again. *Control yourself, woman.* "Will do. Gotta go."

"I'd love to see your dad," he called, but she was already gone. Ben watched her drive away and whistled softly. *They don't make women like Maggie Williams in California.* He'd forgotten what he'd been missing.

Get your copy of *Emma's Dream* today!

ALSO BY M. LEE PRESCOTT

Contemporary Romance

Morgan's Run Romances

Book 1: *Emma's Dream*

Book 2: *Lang's Return*

Book 3: *Jeb's Promise*

Book 4: *Rose's Choice*

Book 5: *Hope's Wonder*

Book 6: *Ruthie's Love*

Book 7: *Polly's Heart*

Book 8: *Kyle's Journey*

Book 9: *Gus' Home*

Book 10: *A Valley Christmas*

Book 11: *Aria's Song*

Morgan's Fire Romances

Book 1: *Lucy's Hearth*

Book 2: *Tim's Hands*

Book 3: *Pam's Garden*

Book 4: *Rich's Dilemma*

Book 5: *Lolly's Wish*

Well-Loved Romances

Widow's Island

Hestor's Way

Mystery

The Ricky Steele Mysteries

Book 1: *Prepped to Kill*

Book 2: *Gadfly*

Book 3: *Lost in Spindle City*

Book 4: *Poof!*

Also, featuring Ricky Steele:

Jigsaw

Roger and Bess Mysteries

Book 1: *A Friend of Silence*

Book 2: *In the Name of Silence*

Book 3: *The Silence of Memory*

Book 4: *Silencing the Pen* (coming in 2021!)

Young Adult Historical Romance

Song of the Spirit

A NOTE FROM THE AUTHOR

I am so happy to bring you Lolly and Jack's love story! This marks the fifth of the *Morgan's Fire* books and also previews book one of the **Morgan's Run** series, *Emma's Dream,* the title that started it all! A contemporary romance series, **Morgan's Fire** follows Helen, Harriet, Lucy, Gail, Pam, Karen, Lolly, and a host of strong, resilient women—and men—across the country to the New England coastal town of Horseshoe Crab Cove.

Thank you so much for reading *Lolly's Wish* and returning to Horseshoe Crab Cove with me. I love this beautiful *fictional* village and the colorful, vibrant characters who inhabit it. If you like *Lolly's Wish* and are willing to write an Amazon review, I would be very grateful. If you would like to sign up for future book releases, giveaways, and occasional notices about my books, please visit *http://www.mleeprescott.com/* and sign up for my newsletter, then follow me on BookBub at *https://www.bookbub.com/search/authors?search=M.+Lee+Prescott*. I promise I will not share your address, nor will I flood you with emails. Do visit my site to read more about my books and hear what's next.

Finally, this book has been revised, proofed, and edited many, many times, but my intrepid assistants and I are human, so if you spot a typo, please email me at *mleeprescott@gmail.com,* and I will fix it. If you'd like to know more about my other books, please scroll ahead to the next section.

Warm wishes,

M. Lee

M. Lee Prescott is the author of dozens of works of fiction for adults, young adults, and children, among them *Prepped to Kill*, *Gadfly*, *Lost in Spindle City*, and *Poof!* (Ricky Steele Mysteries), *A Friend of Silence*, *In the Name of Silence*, and *The Silence of Memory* (Roger and Bess Mysteries), *Jigsaw*, and *Song of the Spirit*, and her contemporary romance series, *Morgan's Run*. And now book five of Morgan's Fire, *Lolly's Wish!* In  addition to her fiction, her nonfiction books are published by Heinemann, and she has written numerous articles in the field of literacy education. Lee is a professor of education at a small New England liberal arts college, where she teaches reading and writing pedagogy. Her current research focuses on mindfulness and connections to literacy. She regularly teaches abroad, most recently in Singapore.

Lee has lived in southern California (love those Laguna nights!), Chapel Hill, North Carolina, and various spots in Massachusetts and Rhode Island. Currently, she resides in Massachusetts on a beautiful river, where she canoes, swims, and watches an incredible variety of wildlife pass by. She is the mother of two grown sons and spends lots of time with them, their beautiful wives, and her beloved grandchildren. When not teaching or writing, Lee's passions revolve around family, yoga (Kripalu is a second home), swimming, sharing mindfulness with children and adults, and walking.

Lee loves to hear from readers. Email her at *mleeprescott@gmail.com*, and visit her website to hear the latest and sign up for her newsletters!

Visit my author website and sign up for my newsletter at
http://www.mleeprescott.com.
Follow me on BookBub *https://www.bookbub.com/search/authors?search=M.+Lee+Prescott*!